PENGUIN ARCHIVE

*A Short Guide to*
*Without a Past*

Albert Camus

1913–1960

A PENGUIN SINCE 1960

Albert Camus
*A Short Guide to Towns Without a Past*

Translated by Ellen Conroy Kennedy and Justin O'Brien

PENGUIN ARCHIVE

PENGUIN BOOKS

UK | USA | Canada | Ireland | Australia
India | New Zealand | South Africa

Penguin Books is part of the Penguin Random House group of companies
whose addresses can be found at global.penguinrandomhouse.com.

Penguin Random House UK,
One Embassy Gardens, 8 Viaduct Gardens, London SW11 7BW

penguin.co.uk

Pieces first published in French in *L'Envers et l'Endroit* (1937), *Noces* (1939)
and *L'Été* (1954).
Selected from *Personal Writings*, published in Penguin Classics 2020
This selection published in Penguin Classics 2025
001

Copyright © 1950, 1954, 1958 by Éditions Gallimard
Translation copyright © Hamish Hamilton, Ltd., and Alfred A. Knopf,
a division of Penguin Random House LLC, 1967 and 1968

No part of this book may be used or reproduced in any manner for the
purpose of training artificial intelligence technologies or systems. In accordance
with Article 4(3) of the DSM Directive 2019/790, Penguin Random House
expressly reserves this work from the text and data mining exception.

Set in 12/15pt Dante MT Std
Typeset by Jouve (UK), Milton Keynes
Printed and bound in Great Britain by Clays Ltd, Elcograf S.p.A.

The authorized representative in the EEA is Penguin Random House Ireland,
Morrison Chambers, 32 Nassau Street, Dublin D02 YH68

A CIP catalogue record for this book is available from the British Library

ISBN: 978–0–241–75201–2

Penguin Random House is committed to a sustainable future
for our business, our readers and our planet. This book is made from
Forest Stewardship Council® certified paper.

# Contents

| | |
|---|---:|
| Love of Life | 1 |
| Nuptials at Tipasa | 9 |
| Summer in Algiers | 19 |
| The Desert | 37 |
| The Minotaur, or Stopping in Oran | 55 |
| Sports | 69 |
| A Short Guide to Towns Without a Past | 89 |
| Return to Tipasa | 97 |

*Love of Life*

At night in Palma, life recedes slowly toward the tune-filled café district behind the market: the streets are dark and silent until one comes upon latticed doorways where light and music filter through. I spent almost a whole night in one of these cafés. It was a small, very low room, rectangular, painted green and hung with pink garlands. The wooden ceiling was covered with tiny red light bulbs. Miraculously fitted into this minute space were an orchestra, a bar with multicolored bottles, and customers squeezed shoulder to shoulder so tight they could hardly breathe. Just men. In the middle, two square yards of free space. Glasses and bottles streamed by as the waiter carried them to all four corners of the room. No one was completely sober. Everyone was shouting. Some sort of naval officer was belching alcohol-laden compliments into my face. An ageless dwarf at my table was telling me his life story. But I was too tense to listen. The orchestra was playing tunes one could only catch the rhythm of, since it was beaten out by every foot in the place. Sometimes the door would open. In the midst of shouts, a new arrival would be fitted in between two chairs.*

Suddenly, the cymbals clashed, and a woman leaped swiftly into the tiny circle in the middle of the cabaret. 'Twenty-one,' the officer told me. I was stupefied. The face of a young girl, but carved in a mountain of flesh. She might have been six feet tall. With all her fat she must have weighed three hundred pounds. Hands on her hips, wearing a yellow net through which a checkerboard of white flesh swelled, she was smiling; and each corner of her mouth sent a series of small ripples of flesh moving toward her ears. The excitement in the room knew no bounds. One felt this girl was known, loved, expected. She was still smiling. She looked around at the customers, still silent and smiling, and wiggled her belly forward. The crowd roared, then demanded a song that everyone seemed to know. It was a nasal Andalusian tune accompanied by a strong three-beat rhythm from the drums. She sang, and at each beat mimed the act of love with her whole body. In this monotonous and passionate

---

* There is a certain freedom of enjoyment that defines true civilization. And the Spanish are among the few peoples in Europe who are civilized.

## Love of Life

movement, real waves of flesh rose from her hips and moved upward until they died away on her shoulders. The room seemed stunned. But pivoting around with the refrain, seizing her breasts with both hands and opening her red, moist mouth, the girl took up the tune in chorus with the audience, until everyone stood upright in the tumult.

As she stood in the center, feet apart, sticky with sweat, hair hanging loose, she lifted her immense torso, which burst forth from its yellow netting. Like an unclean goddess rising from the waves, her eyes hollow, her forehead low and stupid, only a slight quivering at her knees, like a horse's after a race, showed she was still living. In the midst of the foot-stamping joy around her, she was like an ignoble and exalting image of life, with despair in her empty eyes and thick sweat on her belly . . .

Without cafés and newspapers, it would be difficult to travel. A paper printed in our own language, a place to rub shoulders with others in the evenings enable us to imitate the familiar gestures of the man we were at home, who, seen from a distance, seems so much a stranger. For what gives value to travel is fear. It breaks down a kind of inner structure we have. One can no longer cheat – hide behind the hours spent at the office or at the plant (those hours we protest so loudly, which protect us so well from the pain of being alone). I have always wanted to write novels in which my heroes would say: 'What would I do without the office?' or again: 'My wife has died, but fortunately I have all these orders to fill for tomorrow.' Travel robs us of such refuge. Far from our own people, our own language, stripped of all our props, deprived of our masks (one doesn't know the fare on the streetcars, or anything else), we are completely on the surface of ourselves. But also, soul-sick, we restore to every being and every object its miraculous value. A woman dancing without a thought in her head, a bottle on a table, glimpsed behind a curtain: each image becomes a symbol. The whole of life seems reflected in it, insofar as it summarizes our own life at the moment. When we are aware of every gift, the contradictory intoxications we can enjoy (including that of lucidity) are indescribable. Never perhaps has any land but the Mediterranean carried me so far from myself and yet so near.

The emotion I felt at the café in Palma probably came from this. On the other hand, what struck me in the empty district near the cathedral, at noon, among the old palaces with their cool courtyards, in the streets with their scented shadows, was the idea of a certain 'slowness'. No one in the streets. Motionless old women in the miradors. And, walking along past the houses, stopping in courtyards full of green plants and round, gray pillars, I melted into this smell of silence, losing my limits, becoming nothing more than the sound of my footsteps or the flight of birds whose shadows I could see on the still-sunlit portion of the walls. I would also spend long hours in the little Gothic cloister of San Francisco. Its delicate, precious colonnade shone with the fine, golden yellow of old Spanish monuments. In the courtyard there were rose laurels, fake pepper plants, a wrought-iron well from which hung a long, rusty metal spoon. Passers-by drank from it. I still remember sometimes the clear sound it made as it dropped back on the stone of the well. Yet it was not the sweetness of life that this cloister taught me. In the sharp sound of wingbeats as the pigeons flew away, the sudden, snug silence in the middle of the garden, in the lonely squeaking of the chain on its well, I found a new and yet familiar flavor. I was lucid and smiling before this unique play of appearances. A single gesture, I felt, would be enough to shatter this crystal in which the world's face was smiling. Something would come undone – the flight of pigeons would die and each would slowly tumble on its outstretched wings. Only my silence and immobility lent plausibility to what looked so like an illusion. I joined in the game.

I accepted the appearances without being taken in. A fine, golden sun gently warmed the yellow stones of the cloister. A woman was drawing water from the well. In an hour, a minute, a second, now perhaps, everything might collapse. And yet this miracle continued. The world lived on, modest, ironic, and discreet (like certain gentle and reserved forms of women's friendship). A balance continued, colored, however, by all the apprehension of its own end.

There lay all my love of life: a silent passion for what would perhaps escape me, a bitterness beneath a flame. Each day I would leave this cloister like a man lifted from himself, inscribed for a brief moment in the continuance of the world. And I know why I thought then of the expressionless eyes of Doric Apollos or the stiff, motionless characters in Giotto's paintings.* It was at these moments that I truly understood what countries like this could offer me. I am surprised men can find certainties and rules for life on the shores of the Mediterranean, that they can satisfy their reason there and justify optimism and social responsibility. For what struck me then was not a world made to man's measure, but one

---

* The decadence of Greek sculpture and the dispersion of Italian art begin with the appearance of smiles and expression in the eyes, as if beauty ended where the mind begins.

## Love of Life

that closed in upon him. If the language of these countries harmonized with what echoed deeply within me, it was not because it answered my questions but because it made them superfluous. Instead of prayers of thanksgiving rising to my lips, it was this *Nada* whose birth is possible only at the sight of landscapes crushed by the sun. There is no love of life without despair of life.

In Ibiza, I sat every day in the cafés that dot the harbor. Toward five in the evening, the young people would stroll back and forth along the full length of the jetty; this is where marriages and the whole of life are arranged. One cannot help thinking there is a certain grandeur in beginning one's life this way, with the whole world looking on. I would sit down, still dizzy from the day's sun, my head full of white churches and chalky walls, dry fields and shaggy olive trees. I would drink a sweetish syrup, gazing at the curve of the hills in front of me. They sloped gently down to the sea. The evening would grow green. On the largest of the hills, the last breeze turned the sails of a windmill. And, by a natural miracle, everyone lowered his voice. Soon there was nothing but the sky and musical words rising toward it, as if heard from a great distance. There was something fleeting and melancholy in the brief moment of dusk, perceptible not only to one man but also to a whole people. As for me, I longed to love as people long to cry. I felt that every hour I slept now would be an hour stolen from life . . . that is to say, from those hours of undefined desire. I was tense and motionless, as I had been during those vibrant hours at the cabaret in Palma and at the cloister in San Francisco, powerless against this immense desire to hold the world between my hands.

I know that I am wrong, that we cannot give ourselves completely. Otherwise, we could not create. But there are no limits to loving, and what does it matter to me if I hold things badly if I can embrace everything? There are women in Genoa whose smile I loved for a whole morning. I shall never see them again and certainly nothing is simpler. But words will never smother the flame of my regret. I watched the pigeons flying past the little well at the cloister in San Francisco, and forgot my thirst. But a moment always came when I was thirsty again.

## *Nuptials at Tipasa*

In the spring, Tipasa is inhabited by gods and the gods speak in the sun and the scent of absinthe leaves, in the silver armor of the sea, in the raw blue sky, the flower-covered ruins, and the great bubbles of light among the heaps of stone. At certain hours of the day the countryside is black with sunlight. The eyes try in vain to perceive anything but drops of light and colors trembling on the lashes. The thick scent of aromatic plants tears at the throat and suffocates in the vast heat. Far away, I can just make out the black bulk of the Chenoua, rooted in the hills around the village, moving with a slow and heavy rhythm until finally it crouches in the sea.

The village we pass through to get there already opens on the bay. We enter a blue and yellow world and are welcomed by the pungent, odorous sigh of the Algerian summer earth. Everywhere, pinkish bougainvillaea hangs over villa walls; in the gardens the hibiscus are still pale red, and there is a profusion of tea roses thick as cream, with delicate borders of long, blue iris. All the stones are warm. As we step off the buttercup-yellow bus, butchers in their little red trucks are making their morning rounds, calling to the villagers with their horns.

To the left of the port, a drystone stairway leads to the ruins, through the mastic trees and broom. The path goes by a small lighthouse before plunging into the open country. Already, at the foot of this lighthouse, large red, yellow, and violet plants descend toward the first rocks, sucked at by the sea with a kissing sound. As we stand in the slight breeze, with the sun warming one side of our faces, we watch the light coming down from the sky, the smooth sea and the smile of its glittering teeth. We are spectators for the last time before we enter the kingdom of ruins.

After a few steps, the smell of absinthe seizes one by the throat. The wormwood's gray wool covers the ruins as far as the eye can see. Its oil ferments in the heat, and the whole earth gives off a heady alcohol that makes the sky flicker. We walk toward an encounter with love and desire. We are not seeking lessons or the bitter philosophy one requires of greatness. Everything seems futile here except the sun, our kisses, and the wild scents of the earth. I do not seek solitude. I have often been here with those I loved and read on their features the clear smile the

## Nuptials at Tipasa

face of love assumes. Here, I leave order and moderation to others. The great free love of nature and the sea absorbs me completely. In this marriage of ruins and springtime, the ruins have become stones again, and losing the polish imposed on them by men, they have reverted to nature. To celebrate the return of her prodigal daughters Nature has laid out a profusion of flowers. The heliotrope pushes its red and white head between the flagstones of the forum, red geraniums spill their blood over what were houses, temples, and public squares. Like the men whom much knowledge brings back to God, many years have brought these ruins back to their mother's house. Today, their past has finally left them, and nothing distracts them from the deep force pulling them back to the center of all that falls.

How many hours have I spent crushing absinthe leaves, caressing ruins, trying to match my breathing with the world's tumultuous sighs! Deep among wild scents and concerts of somnolent insects, I open my eyes and heart to the unbearable grandeur of this heat-soaked sky. It is not so easy to become what one is, to rediscover one's deepest measure. But watching the solid backbone of the Chenoua, my heart would grow calm with a strange certainty. I was learning to breathe, I was fitting into things and fulfilling myself. As I climbed one after another of the hills, each brought a reward, like the temple whose columns measure the course of the sun and from which one can see the whole village, its white and pink walls and green verandas. Like the basilica on the East hill too, which still has its walls and is surrounded by a great circle of uncovered ornamented coffins, most of them scarcely out of the earth, whose nature they still share. They used to contain corpses; now sage and wallflowers grow in them. The Sainte-Salsa basilica is Christian, but each time we look out through a gap in the walls we are greeted by the song of the world: hillsides planted with pine and cypress trees, or the sea rolling its white horses twenty yards away. The hill on which Sainte-Salsa is built has a flat top and the wind blows more strongly through the portals. Under the morning sun, a great happiness hovers in space.

Those who need myths are indeed poor. Here the gods serve as beds or resting places as the day races across the sky. I describe and say: 'This is red, this blue, this green. This is the sea, the mountain, the flowers.' Need I mention Dionysus to say that I love to crush mastic bulbs under my nose? Is the old hymn that will later come to me quite spontaneously even addressed to Demeter: 'Happy is he alive who has seen these things on earth'? How can we forget the lesson of sight and seeing on this earth? All men

## Nuptials at Tipasa

had to do at the mysteries of Eleusis was watch. Yet even here, I know that I shall never come close enough to the world. I must be naked and dive into the sea, still scented with the perfumes of the earth, wash them off in the sea, and consummate with my flesh the embrace for which sun and sea, lips to lips, have so long been sighing. I feel the shock of the water, rise up through a thick, cold glue, then dive back with my ears ringing, my nose streaming, and the taste of salt in my mouth. As I swim, my arms shining with water flash into gold in the sunlight, until I fold them in again with a twist of all my muscles; the water streams along my body as my legs take tumultuous possession of the waves – and the horizon disappears. On the beach, I flop down on the sand, yield to the world, feel the weight of flesh and bones, again dazed with sunlight, occasionally glancing at my arms where the water slides off and patches of salt and soft blond hair appear on my skin.

Here I understand what is meant by glory: the right to love without limits. There is only one love in this world. To clasp a woman's body is also to hold in one's arms this strange joy that descends from sky to sea. In a moment, when I throw myself down among the absinthe plants to bring their scent into my body, I shall know, appearances to the contrary, that I am fulfilling a truth which is the sun's and which will also be my death's. In a sense, it is indeed my life that I am staking here, a life that tastes of warm stone, that is full of the sighs of the sea and the rising song of the crickets. The breeze is cool and the sky blue. I love this life with abandon and wish to speak of it boldly: it makes me proud of my human condition. Yet people have often told me: there's nothing to be proud of. Yes, there is: this sun, this sea, my heart leaping with youth, the salt taste of my body and this vast landscape in which tenderness and glory merge in blue and yellow. It is to conquer this that I need my strength and my resources. Everything here leaves me intact, I surrender nothing of myself, and don no mask: learning patiently and arduously how to live is enough for me, well worth all their arts of living.

Shortly before noon, we would come back through the ruins to a little café by the side of the port. How cool was the welcome of a tall glass of iced green mint in the shady room, to heads ringing with colors and the cymbals of the sun! Outside were the sea and the road burning with dust. Seated at the table, I would try to blink my eyelids so as to catch the multicolored dazzle of the white-hot sky. Our faces damp with sweat, but our bodies cool in light clothing, we would flaunt the happy weariness of a day of nuptials with the world.

## Nuptials at Tipasa

The food is bad in this café, but there is plenty of fruit, especially peaches, whose juice drips down your chin as you bite into them. Gazing avidly before me, my teeth closing on a peach, I can hear the blood pounding in my ears. The vast silence of noon hangs over the sea. Every beautiful thing has a natural pride in its own beauty, and today the world is allowing its pride to seep from every pore. Why, in its presence, should I deny the joy of living, as long as I know everything is not included in this joy? There is no shame in being happy. But today the fool is king, and I call those who fear pleasure fools. They've told us so much about pride: you know, Lucifer's sin. Beware, they used to cry, you will lose your soul, and your vital powers. I have in fact learned since that a certain pride . . . But at other times I cannot prevent myself from asserting the pride in living that the whole world conspires to give me. At Tipasa, 'I see' equals 'I believe', and I am not stubborn enough to deny what my hands can touch and my lips caress. I don't feel the need to make it into a work of art, but to describe it, which is different. Tipasa seems to me like a character one describes in order to give indirect expression to a certain view of the world. Like such characters, Tipasa testifies to something, and does it like a man. Tipasa is the personage I'm describing today, and it seems to me that the very act of caressing and describing my delight will ensure that it has no end. There is a time for living and a time for giving expression to life. There is also a time for creating, which is less natural. For me it is enough to live with my whole body and bear witness with my whole heart. Live Tipasa, manifest its lessons, and the work of art will come later. Herein lies a freedom.

I never spent more than a day at Tipasa. A moment always comes when one has looked too long at a landscape, just as it is a long time before one sees enough of it. Mountains, the sky, the sea are like faces whose barrenness or splendor we discover by looking rather than seeing. But in order to be eloquent every face must be seen anew. One complains of growing tired too quickly, when one ought to be surprised that the world seems new only because we have forgotten it.

Toward evening I would return to a more formal section of the park, set out as a garden, just off the main road. Leaving the tumult of scents and sunlight, in the cool evening air, the mind would grow calm and the body relaxed, savoring the inner silence born of satisfied love. I would sit on a bench, watching the countryside expand with light. I was full. Above me drooped a pomegranate tree, its flower buds closed and ribbed like small tight fists containing every hope of spring. There was rosemary behind me, and I could smell only the scent of its alcohol. The hills were framed with trees, and beyond them stretched a band of sea on which the sky, like a sail becalmed, rested in all its tenderness. I felt a strange joy in my heart, the special joy that stems from a clear conscience. There is a feeling actors have when they know they've played their part well, that is to say, when they have made their own gestures coincide with those of the ideal character they embody, having entered somehow into a prearranged design, bringing it to life with their own heartbeats. That was exactly what I felt: I had played my part well. I had performed my task as a man, and the fact that I had known joy for one entire day seemed to me not an exceptional success but the intense fulfillment of a condition which, in certain circumstances, makes it our duty to be happy. Then we are alone again, but satisfied.

Now the trees were filled with birds. The earth would give a long sigh before sliding into darkness. In a moment, with the first star, night would fall on the theater of the world. The dazzling gods of day would return to their daily death. But other gods would come.

And, though they would be darker, their ravaged faces too would come from deep within the earth.

For the moment at least, the waves' endless crashing against the shore came toward me through a space dancing with golden pollen. Sea, landscape, silence, scents of this earth, I would drink my fill of a scent-laden life, sinking my teeth into the world's fruit, golden already, overwhelmed by the feeling of its strong, sweet juice flowing on my lips. No, it was neither I nor the world that counted, but solely the harmony and silence that gave birth to the love between us. A love I was not foolish enough to claim for myself alone, proudly aware that I shared it with a whole race born in the sun and sea, alive and spirited, drawing greatness from its simplicity, and upright on the beaches, smiling in complicity at the brilliance of its skies.

## Summer in Algiers

TO JACQUES HEURGON

They are often secret, the love affairs we have with cities. Old towns like Paris, Prague, and even Florence are closed in upon themselves in such a way as to delimit their domain. But Algiers and a few other privileged coastal towns open into the sky like a mouth or a wound. What one can fall in love with in Algiers is what everybody lives with: the sea, visible from every corner, a certain heaviness of the sunlight, the beauty of the people. And, as usual, such generosity and lack of shame emit a more secret perfume. In Paris, one can yearn for space and for the beating of wings. Here, at least, man has everything he needs, and his desires thus assured, can take the measure of his riches.

One probably has to live a long time in Algiers to understand how desiccating an excess of nature's blessings can be. There is nothing here for people seeking knowledge, education, or self-improvement.

The land contains no lessons. It neither promises nor reveals anything. It is content to give, but does so profusely. Everything here can be seen with the naked eye, and is known the very moment it is enjoyed. The pleasures have no remedies and their joys remain without hope. What the land needs are clear-sighted souls, that is to say, those without consolation. It asks that we make an act of lucidity as one makes an act of faith. A strange country, which gives the men it nourishes both their splendor and their misery. It is not surprising that the sensual riches this country offers so profusely to the sensitive person should coincide with the most extreme deprivation. There is no truth that does not also carry bitterness. Why then should it be surprising if I never love the face of this country more than in the midst of its poorest inhabitants?

Throughout their youth, men find a life here that matches their beauty. Decline and forgetfulness come later. They have wagered on the flesh, knowing they would lose. In Algiers, to the young and vital everything is a refuge and a pretext for rejoicing: the bay, the sun, games on the red and white terraces overlooking the sea, the flowers and stadiums, the cool-limbed girls. But for the man who has lost his youth there is nothing to hang on to, and no outlet for melancholy. Elsewhere – on Italian terraces, in

European cloisters, or in the shape of the hills in Provence – there are places where a man can shed his humanity and gently find salvation from himself. But everything here demands solitude and young blood. On his deathbed, Goethe called for light, and this is a historic remark. In Belcourt and Bab-el-Oued, old men sitting at the back of cafés listen to the young, with brilliantined hair, boasting of their exploits.

It is summer in Algiers that grants us these beginnings and these endings. During the summer months, the town is deserted. But the poor and the sky remain. We go down with them to the harbor and its treasures: the water's gentle warmth and the women's brown bodies. In the evening, swollen with these riches, the people return to oilcloth and kerosene lamp, the meager furniture of their existence.

In Algiers, you don't talk about 'going swimming' but about 'knocking off a swim'. I won't insist. People swim in the harbor and then go rest on the buoys. When you pass a buoy where a pretty girl is sitting, you shout to your friends: 'I tell you it's a seagull.' These are healthy pleasures. They certainly seem ideal to the young men, since most of them continue this life during the winter, stripping down for a frugal lunch in the sun at noontime every day. Not that they have read the boring sermons of our nudists, those protestants of the body (there is a way of systematizing the body that is as exasperating as systems for the soul). They just 'like being in the sun'. It would be hard to exaggerate the significance of this custom in our day. For the first time in two thousand years the body has been shown naked on the beaches. For twenty centuries, men have strived to impose decency on the insolence and simplicity of the Greeks, to diminish the flesh and elaborate our dress. Today, reaching back over this history, young men sprinting on the Mediterranean beaches are rediscovering the magnificent motion of the athletes of Delos. Living so close to other bodies, and through one's own body, one finds it has its own nuances, its own life, and, to venture an absurdity, its own psychology.* The evolution of the body, like that

---

\* May I be foolish enough to say that I don't like the way Gide exalts the body? He asks it to hold back desire in order to make it more intense. This brings him close to those who, in the slang of brothels, are termed 'weirdies' or 'oddballs'. Christianity also seeks to suspend desire. But, more naturally, sees in this a mortification. My friend Vincent, who is a cooper and junior breast-stroke champion, has an even clearer view of things. He drinks when he is thirsty, if he wants a woman he tries to sleep with her, and would marry her if he loved her (this hasn't happened yet). Then he always says: 'That feels better!' – an energetic summary of the apology one could write for satiety.

## Summer in Algiers

of the mind, has its history, its reversals, its gains, and its losses. With only this nuance: color. Swimming in the harbor in the summertime, you notice that everybody's skin changes at the same time from white to gold, then to brown, and at last to a tobacco hue, the final stage the body can attain in its quest for transformation. Overlooking the harbor is a pattern of white cubes, the Casbah. From water level, people's bodies form a bronzed frieze against the glaring white background of the Arab town. And, as one moves into August and the sun grows stronger, the white of the houses grows more blinding and the skins take on a darker glow. How then can one keep from feeling a part of this dialogue between stone and flesh, keeping pace with the sun and the seasons? One spends whole mornings diving to peals of laughter in splashing water, on long canoe trips paddling around the red and black freighters (the Norwegian ones smell of all sorts of wood, the German ones reek of oil, the ones going from port to port along the coast smell of wine and old casks). At the hour when the sun spills from every corner of the sky, an orange canoe laden with brown bodies carries us home in one mad sprint. And when, suddenly ceasing the rhythmic stroking of its double fruit-colored wings, we glide into the quiet inner harbor, how can I doubt that what I lead across the silken waters is a cargo of tawny gods, in whom I recognize my brothers?

At the other end of town, summer already offers us the contrast of its other wealth: I mean its silences and boredom. These silences do not always have the same quality, depending on whether they occur in shadow or sunlight. There is a noontime silence on the government square. In the shade of the trees that grow along each side, Arabs sell penny glasses of iced lemonade, perfumed with orange blossom. Their cry of 'cool, cool' echoes across the empty square. When it fades away, silence falls again under the sun: ice moves in the merchant's pitcher, and I can hear it tinkling. There is a siesta silence. On the streets around the docks, in front of the squalid barber shops, one can measure it in the melodious buzzing of the flies behind the hollow reed curtains. Elsewhere, in the Moorish cafés of the Casbah, it is bodies that are silent, that cannot drag themselves away, leave the glass of tea, and rediscover time in the beating of their pulse. But, above all, there is the silence of the summer evenings.

These brief moments when day trembles into night must swarm with secret signs and calls to be so closely linked to Algiers in my heart. When I have been away from this country for some time, I think of its twilights as promises of happiness. On the hills

## Summer in Algiers

looking down over the town, there are paths among the mastic and the olive trees. And it is toward them that my heart turns then. I can see sheaves of black birds rising against the green horizon. In the sky, suddenly emptied of its sun, something releases its hold. A whole flock of tiny red clouds stretches upward until it dissolves into the air. Almost immediately afterward appears the first star, which had been taking shape and growing harder in the thickness of the heavens. And then, sudden and all-enveloping, the night. What is so unique in these fleeting evenings of Algiers that they free so many things in me? They leave a sweetness on my lips that vanishes into the night before I have time to weary of it. Is this the secret of their persistence? The tenderness of this country is overwhelming and furtive. But at least our heart gives way to it completely. The dance hall at Padovani Beach is open every day. And, in this immense rectangular box, open to the sea all along one side, the poor youngsters of the district come to dance until evening. Often, I would wait there for one particular moment. In the daytime, the dance hall is protected by a sloping wooden roof. When the sun has gone down it is removed. The hall fills with a strange green light, born in the double shell of sky and sea. When you sit far from the windows, you can see only the sky, and, like puppets in a shadow theater, the faces of the dancers floating past, one after another. Sometimes they play a waltz, and the dark profiles revolve like cutout figures on a turntable. Night comes quickly and with it the lights. I shall never be able to describe the thrill and the secret enchantment of this subtle moment. I remember a magnificent, tall girl who had danced all one afternoon. She was wearing a necklace of jasmine on her close-fitting blue dress, which was damp with sweat right down the back. She was laughing and throwing back her head as she danced. Passing in front of the tables, she left behind a mingled scent of flowers and flesh. When evening came, I could no longer see her body pressed against her partner, but the white of her jasmine and the black of her hair swirled one after the other against the sky, and when she threw back her breasts I could hear her laugh and see her partner's silhouette lean suddenly forward. I owe my idea of innocence to evenings like these. And I am learning not to separate these beings charged with violence from the sky in which their desires revolve.

At the neighborhood movie houses in Algiers, they sometimes sell pastilles with engraved red mottoes that express everything needed for the birth of love: (A) questions: 'When will you marry me?';'Do you love me?'; (B) replies: 'Madly'; 'Next spring.' After having prepared the ground, you pass them to the girl next to you, who answers in kind or simply plays dumb. At Belcourt, there have been marriages arranged like this, whole lives decided in an exchange of mint candies. And this gives a good picture of the childlike people of this country.

The hallmark of youth, perhaps, is a magnificent vocation for easy pleasures. But, above all, the haste to live borders on extravagance. In Belcourt, as in Bab-el-Oued, people marry young. They start work very early, and exhaust the range of human experience in ten short years. A workingman of thirty has already played all his cards. He waits for the end with his wife and children around him. His delights have been swift and merciless. So has his life. And you understand then that he is born in a land where everything is given to be taken away. In such abundance and profusion, life follows the curve of the great passions, sudden, demanding, generous. It is not meant to be built, but to be burned up. So reflection or self-improvement are quite irrelevant. The notion of hell, for example, is nothing more than an amusing joke here. Only the very virtuous are allowed such fancies. And I even think that virtue is a meaningless word in Algeria. Not that these men lack principles. They have their code of morality, which is very well defined. You 'don't let your mother down'. You see to it that your wife is respected in the street. You show consideration to pregnant women. You don't attack an enemy two to one, because 'that's dirty'. If anyone fails to observe these elementary rules 'He's not a man,' and that's all there is to it. This seems to me just and strong. There are still many of us who observe the highway code, the only disinterested one I know. But at the same time, shopkeeper morality is unknown. I have always seen the faces around me take on an expression of pity at the sight of a man between two policemen. And, before finding out whether the man was a thief, a parricide, or simply an eccentric, people said: 'Poor fellow,' or again, with a touch of admiration: 'He's a real pirate, that one!'

There are people born for pride and for life. It is they who nourish the most singular vocation for boredom, they too who find death the most repulsive. Apart from sensual delights, Algerian amusements are idiotic. A bowling club, fraternal society dinners, cheap movies, and communal celebrations have for years now been enough to keep the over-thirty age group entertained. Sundays in Algiers are among the dreariest anywhere. How would these mindless people know how to disguise the deep horror of their lives with myths? In

## Summer in Algiers

Algiers, everything associated with death is either ridiculous or detestable. The people have neither religion nor idols and die alone after having lived in a crowd. I know no place more hideous than the cemetery on the boulevard Bru, which is opposite one of the most beautiful landscapes in the world. A fearful sadness rises from the accumulated bad taste of its black monuments, revealing death's true face. 'Everything passes,' the heart-shaped ex-votos read, 'but memory.' And they all insist on the ridiculous eternity provided at so small a price by the hearts of those who loved us. The same phrases serve all forms of despair. They are addressed to the deceased and speak in the second-person singular: 'Our memory will never abandon thee' – a gloomy pretense by means of which one lends a body and desires to what is, at best, a black liquid. In another spot, in the midst of a stupefying display of flowers and marble birds, is this reckless vow: 'Never shall thy grave lack flowers.' But one is quickly reassured: the words are carved around a gilded stucco bouquet, a great timesaver for the living (like those flowers called 'everlasting', which owe their pompous name to the gratitude of those who still jump on moving buses). Since one must move with the times, the classical warbler is sometimes replaced by a breath-taking pearly airplane, piloted by a silly-looking angel who, disregarding all logic, has been provided with a magnificent pair of wings.

Still, how can I explain it, these images of death never quite separate themselves from life? The values are closely linked. The favorite joke of Algerian undertakers, driving by in an empty hearse, is to shout 'like a ride, honey?' to the pretty girls they meet along the way. There is nothing to keep one from finding this symbolic, if in somewhat bad taste. It may also seem blasphemous to greet the news of someone's death with a wink of the left eye and the comment 'Poor guy, he won't sing any more.' Or, like the woman from Oran who had never loved her husband: 'The Lord gave him to me, the Lord hath taken him away.' But when all is said and done, I don't see what is sacred about death, and I am, on the contrary, very aware of the difference between fear and respect. Everything breathes the horror of death in this country that is an invitation to life. And yet it is beneath the walls of this very cemetery that the young men of Belcourt arrange their meetings and the girls let themselves be kissed and fondled.

I fully realize that such people cannot be accepted by everyone. Intelligence does not occupy the place here that it does in Italy. This race is indifferent to the mind. It worships and admires the body. From this comes its strength, its naïve cynicism, and a puerile

## Summer in Algiers

vanity that leads it to be severely criticized. People commonly reproach its 'mentality', that is to say, its particular mode of life and set of values. And it is true that a certain intensity of living involves some injustice. Yet here are a people with no past, with no traditions, though not without poetry. Their poetry has a hard, sensual quality I know very well; it is far from tender, even from the tenderness of the Algerian sky; it is the only poetry, in fact, that moves me and restores me. The opposite of a civilized people is a creative one. These barbarians lounging on the beaches give me the foolish hope that, perhaps without knowing it, they are modeling the face of a culture where man's greatness will finally discover its true visage. These people, wholly engaged in the present, live with neither myths nor consolation. Investing all their assets on this earth, they are left defenseless against death. The gifts of physical beauty have been heaped upon them. And, also, the strange greediness that always goes along with wealth that has no future. Everything people do in Algiers reveals a distaste for stability and a lack of regard for the future. People are in a hurry to live, and if an art were to be born here it would conform to the hatred of permanence that led the Dorians to carve their first column out of wood. And still, yes, one can find a certain moderation as well as a constant excess in the strained and violent faces of these people, in this summer sky emptied of tenderness, beneath which all truths can be told and on which no deceitful divinity has traced the signs of hope or of redemption. Between this sky and the faces turned toward it there is nothing on which to hang a mythology, a literature, an ethic, or a religion – only stones, flesh, stars, and those truths the hand can touch.

To feel one's ties to a land, one's love for certain men, to know there is always a place where the heart can find rest – these are already many certainties for one man's life. Doubtless they are not enough. But at certain moments everything yearns for this homeland of the soul. 'Yes, it is to this we must return.' What is strange about finding on earth the unity Plotinus longed for? Unity expresses itself here in terms of sea and sky. The heart senses it through a certain taste of the flesh that constitutes its bitterness and greatness. I am learning that there is no superhuman happiness, no eternity outside the curve of the days. These ridiculous and essential assets, these relative truths are the only ones that move me. I have not enough soul to understand the other, 'ideal' ones. Not that we should behave as beasts, but I can see no point in the happiness of angels. All I know is that this sky will last longer than

## Summer in Algiers

I shall. And what can I call eternity except what will continue after my death? What I am expressing here is not the creature's complacency about his condition. It is something quite different. It is not always easy to be a man, even less to be a man who is pure. But to be pure means to rediscover that country of the soul where one's kinship with the world can be felt, where the throbbing of one's blood mingles with the violent pulsations of the afternoon sun. It is a well-known fact that we always recognize our homeland at the moment we are about to lose it. Men whose self-torments are too great are those whom their native land rejects. I have no desire to be crude or to seem to exaggerate. But after all, what denies me in this life is first of all what kills me. Everything that exalts life at the same time increases its absurdity. In the Algerian summer I learn that only one thing is more tragic than suffering, and that is the life of a happy man. But this can also be the path to a greater life, since it can teach us not to cheat.

Many people, in fact, affect a love of life in order to avoid love itself. They try to enjoy themselves and 'to experiment'. But this is an intellectual attitude. It takes a rare vocation to become a sensualist. A man lives out his life without the help of his mind, with its triumphs and defeats, its simultaneous loneliness and companionship. Seeing those men from

Belcourt who work, take care of their wives and children, often without a word of complaint, I think that one can feel a certain shame. I certainly have no illusions. There is not much love in the lives I am describing. I should say rather that there is no longer very much. But at least they have eluded nothing. There are some words that I have never really understood, such as sin. Yet I think I know that these men have never sinned against life. For if there is a sin against life, it lies perhaps less in despairing of it than in hoping for another life and evading the implacable grandeur of the one we have. These men have not cheated. They were gods of the summer at twenty in their thirst for life, and they are still gods today, stripped of all hope. I have seen two of them die. They were full of horror, but silent. It is better that way. From the mass of human evils swarming in Pandora's box, the Greeks brought out hope at the very last, as the most terrible of all. I don't know any symbol more moving. For hope, contrary to popular belief, is tantamount to resignation. And to live is not to be resigned.

Such at least is the bitter lesson of summers in Algiers. But already the season trembles and the summer passes. After so much violence and tension, the first September rains are like the first tears of a liberated land, as if for a few days this country were bathed in tenderness. Yet at the same time the carob trees emit the scent of love across Algeria. In the evening or after the rain, the whole earth lies, its belly moistened with a bitter almond-scented seed, at rest from having yielded all summer long to the sun. And once again this fragrance consecrates the nuptials of man and earth, and gives rise in us to the only truly virile love in this world: one that is generous and will die.

## The Desert

TO JEAN GRENIER

Living, of course, is rather the opposite of expressing. If I am to believe the great Tuscan masters, it means bearing triple witness, in silence, fire, and immobility. It takes a long time to realize that one can encounter the faces in these Tuscan paintings any day of the week in the streets of Florence or Pisa. But of course we no longer know how to see the real faces of those around us. We no longer look at our contemporaries, eager only for those points of reference in them that determine our behavior. We prefer its most vulgar poetry to the face itself. As for Giotto and Piero della Francesca, they are perfectly aware that a man's feelings are nothing. Surely everyone has a heart. But the great simple, eternal emotions around which the love of living revolves – hatred, love, tears, and joys – these grow deep inside a man and mold the visage of his destiny, like the grief that makes Mary clench her teeth in Giottino's

'Entombment'. In the immense friezes of Tuscan churches I make out crowds of angels, their features scarcely traced, but in each mute and passionate face I recognize a solitude.

What matters are not picturesque qualities, episodes, shades of color, or emotional effects. What counts is not poetry. What counts is truth. And I call truth anything that continues. There is a subtle lesson in thinking that, in this respect, only painters can satisfy our hunger. This is because they have the privilege of making themselves novelists of the body. Because they work in that magnificent and trivial matter called the present. And the present always shows itself in a gesture. They do not paint a smile, a fleeting moment of modesty, of regret, or of expectation, but a face with the shape of its bones and the warmth of its blood. What they have expelled from these faces molded for eternity is the curse of the mind: at the price of hope. For the body knows nothing of hope. All it knows is the beating of its own heart. Its eternity consists of indifference. As in the 'Scourging of Christ' by Piero della Francesca, where, in a freshly washed courtyard, both the tortured Christ and the thickset executioner reveal the same detachment in their attitudes. This is because the torment has no sequel. Its lesson ends with the frame around the canvas. Why should a man who expects no tomorrow feel emotion? The impassiveness and the greatness that man shows when he has no hope, the eternal present, is precisely what perceptive theologians have called hell. And hell, as everyone knows, also consists of bodily suffering. The Tuscan painters stop at the body and not at its destiny. There are no prophetic paintings. And it is not in museums that we must seek reasons to hope.

The immortality of the soul, it is true, engrosses many noble minds. But this is because they reject the body, the only truth that is given them, before using up its strength. For the body presents no problems, or, at least, they know the only solution it proposes: a truth which must perish and which thus acquires a bitterness and nobility they dare not contemplate directly. Noble minds would rather have poetry than the body, for poetry concerns the soul. Clearly, I am playing on words. But it is also clear that all I wish to do by calling it truth is consecrate a higher poetry: the dark flame that Italian painters from Cimabue to Francesca have raised from the Tuscan landscape as the lucid protestation of men thrown upon an earth whose splendor and light speak ceaselessly to them of a non-existent God.

Sometimes indifference and insensitivity permit a face to merge with the mineral grandeur of a landscape. Just as certain Spanish peasants come to resemble their own olive trees, so the faces in Giotto's pictures, shorn of the insignificant shadows that reveal the soul, finally merge with Tuscany itself in the only lesson it freely offers: the exercise of passion at the expense of feeling, a mixture of asceticism and pleasure, a resonance common to both man and the earth and by which man, like the earth, defines himself as halfway between wretchedness and love. There are not many truths the heart can be sure of. I realized this one evening as the shadows were beginning to drown the vines and olive trees of the Florentine countryside in a vast and silent sadness. But sadness in this country is never anything but a commentary on beauty. And as the train traveled on through the evening I felt a tension in me slowly relaxing. Can I doubt today that even with the face of sadness, one could call it happiness?

Yes, Italy also lavishes on every landscape the lesson illustrated by its men. But it is easy to miss our chance of happiness, for it is always undeserved. The same is true of Italy. And if its grace is sudden, it is not always immediate. More than any other country, Italy invites us to deepen an experience that paradoxically seems to be complete on first acquaintance. This is because it begins by pouring out its poetry the better to disguise its truth. Italy's first enchantments are rites of forgetfulness: the

*The Desert*

laurel roses of Monaco, flower-filled Genoa with its smell of fish, and blue evenings on the Ligurian coast. Then finally Pisa, and with it an Italy which has lost the rather tawdry charm of the Riviera. But it is still a land of easy virtue, so why not lend ourselves for a time to its sensual grace? There is nothing urging me on while I am here (I am deprived of the joys of the harried tourist, since a cheap ticket compels me to spend a certain time in the town 'of my choice'). My patience for love and understanding seems endless on this first evening when, dead tired and starved, I enter Pisa, greeted on the station platform by ten loudspeakers bellowing out a flood of sentimental songs to an almost entirely youthful crowd. I already know what I expect. After the life here has surged around me, the strange moment will come, when, with the cafés closed and the silence suddenly restored, I'll walk through the short, dark streets toward the center of the town. The black and gold Arno, the green and yellow monuments, the empty town – how can I describe the neat and sudden subterfuge that transforms Pisa at ten each evening into a strange stage-set of silence, water, and stone. 'In such a night as this, Jessica!' Here, on this unique stage, gods appear with the voices of Shakespeare's lovers . . . We must learn how to lend ourselves to dreaming when dreams lend themselves to us. Already I can hear in the depth of this Italian night the strains of the more private song that people come to look for here. Tomorrow, and only tomorrow, the countryside will round out in the morning light. Tonight I am a god among gods, and as Jessica flies off 'on the swift steps of love', I mingle my voice with Lorenzo's. But Jessica is only a pretext; this surge of love goes beyond her. Yes, I think Lorenzo is not so much in love with her as grateful to her for allowing him to love. Why should I dream this evening of the lovers of Venice and forget Verona's? Because there is nothing here that invites us to cherish unhappy lovers. Nothing is more vain than to die for love. What we ought to do is live. A living Lorenzo is better than a Romeo in his grave, despite his rosebush. Then why not dance in these celebrations of living love – and sleep in the afternoons on the lawn of the Piazza del Duomo, surrounded by monuments there will always be time enough to visit, drink from the city's fountains where the water is lukewarm but so fluid, and look once more for the face of that laughing woman with the long nose and proud mouth. All we need understand is that this initiation prepares us for higher illuminations. These are the dazzling processions that lead to the Dionysian mysteries at Eleusis. It is in joy that man prepares his lessons and when his ecstasy is at its highest pitch that the flesh becomes conscious and consecrates its communion with a sacred mystery whose symbol is black blood. It is now that the self-forgetfulness drawn from the ardor of that first Italy prepares us for the lesson that frees us from hope and from our history. These twin truths of the body and of the moment, at the spectacle of beauty – how can we not cling to them as to the only happiness we can expect, one that will enchant us but at the same time perish?

The most loathsome materialism is not the kind people usually think of, but the sort that attempts to let dead ideas pass for living realities, diverting into sterile myths the stubborn and lucid attention we give to what we have within us that must forever die. I remember that in Florence, in the cloister of the dead at the Santissima Annunziata, I was carried away by something I mistook for distress, which was only anger. It was raining. I was reading the inscriptions on the tombstones and ex-votos. One man had been a tender father and a faithful husband; another, at the same time the best of husbands and a skillful merchant. A young woman, a model of all the virtues, had spoken French *'si come il native'*. There was a young girl, who had been the hope of her whole family, *'ma la gioia è pellegrina sulla terra'*. None of this affected me. Nearly all of them, according to the inscriptions, had resigned themselves to dying, doubtless because they accepted their other duties. Children had invaded the cloister and were playing leapfrog over the tombstones that strove to perpetuate their virtues. Night was falling, and I had sat down on the ground, my back against a column. A priest smiled at me as he went by. In the church, an organ was playing softly, and the warm color of its pattern sometimes emerged behind the children's shouts. Alone against the column, I was like someone seized by the throat, who shouts out his faith as if it were his last word. Everything in me protested against such a resignation. 'You must,' said the inscriptions. But no, and my revolt was right. This joy that was moving forward, indifferent and absorbed like a pilgrim treading on the earth, was something that I had to follow step by step. And, as to the rest, I said no. I said no with all my strength. The tombstones were teaching me that it was pointless, that life is '*col sol levante, col sol cadente*'. But even today I cannot see what my revolt loses by being pointless, and I am well aware of what it gains.

Besides, that is not what I set out to say. I would like to define a little more clearly a truth I felt then at the very heart of my revolt and of which this revolt was only an extension, a truth that stretched

*The Desert*

from the tiny last roses in the cloister of Santa Maria Novella to the women on that Sunday morning in Florence, their breasts free beneath their light dresses, and their moist lips. On every church corner, that Sunday morning, there were displays of flowers, their petals thick and shining, bejeweled with spots of water. I found in them then a kind of 'simplicity' as well as a reward. There was a generous opulence in the flowers and in the women, and I could not see that desiring the latter was much different from longing for the former. The same pure heart sufficed for both. It's not often a man feels his heart is pure. But when he does, it is his duty to call what has so singularly purified him truth, even if this truth may seem a blasphemy to others, as is the case with what I thought that day. I had spent the morning in a Franciscan convent, at Fiesole, full of the scent of laurel. I had stood for a long time in a little courtyard overflowing with red flowers, sunlight, and black and yellow bees. In one corner there was a green watering can. Earlier, I had visited the monks' cells, and seen their little tables, each adorned with a skull. Now, the garden testified to their inspiration. I had turned back toward Florence, down the hill that led toward the town lying open with all its cypress trees. I felt this splendor of the world, the women and the flowers, was a kind of justification for these men.

I was not sure that they were not also the justification for all men who know that an extreme level of poverty always meets the wealth and luxury of the world. Between the life of these Franciscans enclosed among columns and flowers and the life of the young men of the Padovani beach in Algiers who spend the whole year in the sun, I felt there was a common resonance. If they strip themselves bare, it is for a greater life (and not for another life). At least, that is the only valid meaning of such expressions as 'deprivation' and 'stripping oneself bare'. Being naked always carries a sense of physical liberty and of the harmony between hand and flowers – the loving understanding between the earth and a man delivered from the human – ah! I would be a convert if this were not already my religion. No, what I have just said cannot be a blasphemy – any more than if I say that the inner smile of Giotto's portraits of Saint Francis justifies those who have a taste for happiness. For myths are to religion what poetry is to truth: ridiculous masks laid upon the passion to live.

Shall I go further? The same men at Fiesole who live among red flowers keep in their cells the skull that nourishes their meditations. Florence at their windows and death on their tables. A certain continuity in despair can give birth to joy. And when life reaches a certain temperature, our soul and

## The Desert

our blood mingle and live at ease in contradiction, as indifferent to duty as to faith. I am no longer surprised that a cheerful hand should thus have summarized its strange notion of honor on a wall in Pisa: *'Alberto fa l'amore con la mia sorella.'* I am no longer surprised that Italy should be the land of incest, or at least, what is more significant, of admitted incest. For the path that leads from beauty to immorality is tortuous but certain. Plunged deep in beauty, the mind feeds off nothingness. When a man faces landscapes whose grandeur clutches him by the throat, each movement of his mind is a scratch on his perfection. And soon, crossed out, scarred and rescarred by so many overwhelming certainties, man ceases to be anything at all in the face of the world but a formless stain knowing only passive truths, the world's color or its sun. Landscapes as pure as this dry up the soul and their beauty is unbearable. The message of these gospels of stone, sky, and water is that there are no resurrections. Henceforth, from the depths of the deserts that the heart sees as magnificent, men of these countries begin to feel temptation. Why is it surprising if minds brought up before the spectacle of nobility, in the rarefied air of beauty, remain unconvinced that greatness and goodness can live in harmony. An intelligence with no god to crown its glory seeks for a god in what denies it. Borgia, on his arrival in the Vatican, exclaims: 'Now that God has given us the papacy, let us hasten to enjoy it.' And he behaves accordingly. 'Hasten' is indeed the word. There is already a hint of the despair so characteristic of people who have everything.

Perhaps I am mistaken. For I was in fact happy in Florence, like many others before me. But what is happiness except the simple harmony between a man and the life he leads? And what more legitimate harmony can unite a man with life than the dual consciousness of his longing to endure and his awareness of death? At least he learns to count on nothing and to see the present as the only truth given to us 'as a bonus'. I realize that people talk about Italy, the Mediterranean, as classical countries where everything is on a human scale. But where is this, and where is the road that leads the way? Let me open my eyes to seek my measure and my satisfaction! What I see is Fiesole, Djemila, and ports in the sunlight. The human scale? Silence and dead stones. All the rest belongs to history.

And yet this is not the end. For no one has said that happiness should be forever inseparable from optimism. It is linked to love – which is not the same thing. And I know of times and places where happiness can seem so bitter that we prefer the promise

## The Desert

of it. But this is because at such times or places I had not heart enough to love – that is, to persevere in love. What we must talk of here is man's entry into the celebration of beauty and the earth. For now, like the neophyte shedding his last veils, he surrenders to his god the small change of his personality. Yes, there is a higher happiness, where happiness seems trivial. In Florence, I climbed right to the top of the Boboli gardens, to a terrace from which I could see Mount Oliveto and the upper part of the town as far as the horizon. On each of the hills, the olive trees were pale as little wisps of smoke, and the stronger shoots of the cypresses stood out against their light mist, the nearer ones green and the further ones black. Heavy clouds spotted the deep blue of the sky. As the afternoon drew to a close, a silvery light bathed everything in silence. At first the hilltops had been hidden in clouds. But a breeze had risen whose breath I could feel on my cheek. As it blew, the clouds behind the mountains drew apart like two sides of a curtain. At the same time, the cypress trees on the summit seemed to shoot up in a single jet against the sudden blue of the sky. With them, the whole hillside and landscape of stones and olive trees rose slowly back into sight. Other clouds appeared. The curtain closed. And the hill with its cypress trees and houses vanished once more. Then the same breeze, which was closing the thick folds of the curtain over other hills, scarcely visible in the distance, came and pulled them open here anew. As the world thus filled and emptied its lungs, the same breath ended a few seconds away and then, a little further off, took up again the theme of a fugue that stone and air were playing on a world-scale. Each time, the theme was repeated in a slightly lower key. As I followed it into the distance, I became a little calmer. Reaching the end of so stirring a vision, with one final glance I took in the whole range of hills breathing in unison as they slipped away, as if in some song of the entire earth.

Millions of eyes, I knew, had gazed at this landscape, and for me it was like the first smile of the sky. It took me out of myself in the deepest sense of the word. It assured me that but for my love and the wondrous cry of these stones, there was no meaning in anything. The world is beautiful, and outside it there is no salvation. The great truth that it patiently taught me is that the mind is nothing, nor even the heart. And that the stone warmed by the sun or the cypress tree shooting up against the suddenly clear sky mark the limits of the only universe in which 'being right' is meaningful: nature without men. And this world annihilates me. It carries me to the end. It denies me without anger. As that evening fell

## The Desert

over Florence, I was moving toward a wisdom where everything had already been overcome, except that tears came into my eyes and a great sob of poetry welling up within me made me forget the world's truth.

It is on this moment of balance I must end: the strange moment when spirituality rejects ethics, when happiness springs from the absence of hope, when the mind finds its justification in the body. If it is true that every truth carries its bitterness within, it is also true that every denial contains a flourish of affirmations. And this song of hopeless love born in contemplation may also seem the most effective guide for action. As he emerges from the tomb, the risen Christ of Piero della Francesca has no human expression on his face – only a fierce and soulless grandeur that I cannot help taking for a resolve to live. For the wise man, like the idiot, expresses little. The reversion delights me.

But do I owe this lesson to Italy, or have I drawn it from my own heart? It was surely in Italy that I became aware of it. But this is because Italy, like other privileged places, offers me the spectacle of a beauty in which, nonetheless, men die. Here again truth must decay, and what is more exalting? Even if I long for it, what have I in common with a truth that is not destined to decay? It is not on my scale. And to love it would be pretense. People rarely understand that it is never through despair that a man gives up what constituted his life. Impulses and moments of despair lead toward other lives and merely indicate a quivering attachment to the lessons of the earth. But it can happen that when he reaches a certain degree of lucidity a man feels his heart is closed, and without protest or rebellion turns his back on what up to then he had taken for his life, that is to say, his restlessness. If Rimbaud dies in Abyssinia without having written a single line, it is not because he prefers adventure or has renounced literature. It is because 'that's how things are', and because when we reach a certain stage of awareness we finally acknowledge something which each of us, according to our particular vocation, seeks not to understand. This clearly involves undertaking the survey of a certain desert. But this strange desert is accessible only to those who can live there in the full anguish of their thirst. Then, and only then, is it peopled with the living waters of happiness.

Within reach of my hand, in the Boboli gardens, hung enormous golden Chinese persimmons whose bursting skin oozed a thick syrup. Between this light hill and these juicy fruits, between the secret brotherhood linking me to the world and the hunger urging

## The Desert

me to seize the orange-colored flesh above my hand, I could feel the tension that leads certain men from asceticism to sensual delights and from self-denial to the fullness of desire. I used to wonder, I still wonder at this bond that unites man with the world, this double image in which my heart can intervene and dictate its happiness up to the precise limit where the world can either fulfill or destroy it. Florence! One of the few places in Europe where I have understood that at the heart of my revolt consent is dormant. In its sky mingled with tears and sunlight, I learned to consent to the earth and be consumed in the dark flame of its celebrations. I felt . . . but what word can I use? What excess? How can one consecrate the harmony of love and revolt? The earth! In this great temple deserted by the gods, all my idols have feet of clay.

## *The Minotaur, or Stopping in Oran*

TO PIERRE GALINDO

This essay dates from 1939 – something the reader should bear in mind in judging what Oran might be like today. Violent protests emanating from this beautiful town have in fact assured me that all the imperfections have been (or will be) remedied. The beauties celebrated in this essay, have, on the other hand, been jealously protected. Oran, a happy and realistic city, no longer needs writers. It is waiting for tourists.

(1953)

There are no more deserts. There are no more islands. Yet one still feels the need of them. To understand this world, one must sometimes turn away from it; to serve men better, one must briefly hold them at a distance. But where can the necessary solitude be found, the long breathing space in which the mind gathers its strength and takes stock of its courage? There are still the great cities. But they must meet certain conditions.

The cities Europe offers are too full of murmurs from the past. A practiced ear can still detect the rustling of wings, the quivering of souls. We feel the dizziness of the centuries, of glory and revolutions. We are reminded of the clamor in which Europe was forged. There is not enough silence.

Paris is often a desert for the heart, but sometimes, from the height of Père-Lachaise, a wind of revolution suddenly fills this desert with flags and vanquished grandeurs. The same is true of certain Spanish towns, of Florence or Prague. Salzburg would be peaceful without Mozart. But now and then the great cry of Don Juan plunging into hell runs across the Salzach. Vienna seems more silent, a maiden among cities. Its stones are no more than three centuries old, and their youth has known no sadness. But Vienna stands at a crossroads of history. The clash of empires echoes around her. On certain evenings when the sky clothes itself in blood, the stone horses on the monuments of the Ring seem about to take flight. In this fleeting instant, when everything speaks of power and history, you can distinctly hear the Ottoman empire crashing under the charge of the Polish cavalry. Here, too, there is not enough silence.

It is certainly this well-populated solitude that

## The Minotaur, or Stopping in Oran

men look for in the cities of Europe. At least, men who know what they want. Here, they can choose their company, take it and leave it. How many minds have been tempered in the walk between a hotel room and the old stones of the Île Saint-Louis! It is true that others died of loneliness. But it was here, in any case, that those who survived found reasons to grow and for self-affirmation. They were alone and yet not alone. Centuries of history and beauty, the burning evidence of a thousand past lives, accompanied them along the Seine and spoke to them both of traditions and of conquests. But their youth urged them to call forth this company. There comes a time, there come times in history, when such company is a nuisance. 'It's between the two of us now,' cries Rastignac as he confronts the vast mustiness of Paris. Yes, but two can also be too many!

Deserts themselves have taken on a meaning; poetry has handicapped them. They have become the sacred places for all the world's suffering. What the heart requires at certain moments is just the opposite, a place without poetry. Descartes, for his meditations, chose as his desert the busiest commercial city of his time. There he found his solitude, and the chance to write what is perhaps the greatest of our virile poems: 'The first (precept) was never to accept anything as true unless I knew without the slightest doubt that it was so.' One can have less ambition and yet the same longing. But for the last three centuries Amsterdam has been covered with museums. To escape from poetry and rediscover the peacefulness of stones we need other deserts, and other places without soul or resources. Oran is one of these.

## THE STREET

I have often heard people from Oran complain about their town: 'There are no interesting people here.' But you wouldn't want them if there were! A number of high-minded people have tried to acclimate this desert to the customs of another world, faithful to the principle that no one can genuinely serve art or ideas without cooperation from others.* The result is that the only edifying circles are those of poker players, boxing and bowling fans, and local clubs. At least their atmosphere is natural. After all, there is a kind of greatness that doesn't lend itself to elevation. It is sterile by nature. And anyone who wants to find it leaves the clubs behind to descend into the street.

---

* In Oran, you meet Gogol's Klestakoff. He yawns and then says: 'I feel we ought to concern ourselves with higher things.'

## *The Minotaur, or Stopping in Oran*

The streets of Oran are reserved for dust, pebbles, and heat. If it rains there is a flood and a sea of mud. But rain or shine, the shops have the same absurd, extravagant look. All the bad taste of Europe and the Orient meets in Oran. There, pell-mell, are marble greyhounds, Swan Lake ballet dancers, Diana the Huntress in green galalith, discus throwers and harvesters, everything that serves as wedding or birthday presents, the whole depressing crew that some joker of a businessman endlessly conjures up to fill our mantelpieces. But the relentless bad taste reaches a point of baroque extravagance where all can be forgiven. Behold, embellished with dust, the contents of one shop window: ghastly plaster-cast models of tortured feet, a batch of Rembrandt sketches 'given away at 150 francs each', a quantity of 'practical jokes and tricks', tricolor wallets, an eighteenth-century pastel drawing, a mechanical plush donkey, bottles of *eau de Provence* for preserving green olives, and a wretched wooden Virgin with an indecent smile. (So that no one will be left in ignorance, the management has placed a label at its feet: 'Wooden Virgin'.)

You can find in Oran:

1. Cafés whose grease-covered countertops are strewn with the feet and wings of flies, where the proprietor never stops smiling although the place is always

empty. A 'small black coffee' used to cost twelve sous and a 'large' eighteen;

2. Photographers' shops where techniques have not progressed since the invention of sensitized paper. They display a singular fauna, never encountered in the street, ranging from a pseudo sailor leaning with one elbow on a console table to a marriageable maiden in a dowdy dress, simpering with dangling arms against a sylvan background. It can be assumed that these are not copies from nature but original creations;

3. An edifying abundance of undertakers. This is not because more people die in Oran than elsewhere, but simply, I suppose, because they make more fuss about it.

The endearing simplicity of this nation of shopkeepers even extends to their advertising. The program of a local movie theater describes a third-rate coming attraction. I note the adjectives 'magnificent', 'splendid', 'extraordinary', 'marvelous', 'overwhelming', and 'stupendous'. In conclusion, the management informs the public of the considerable sacrifices it has had to make in order to be able to present this astonishing production. The price of seats, however, will remain the same.

It would be wrong to assume that this merely

## The Minotaur, or Stopping in Oran

shows the taste for exaggeration peculiar to Mediterranean countries. What the authors of this remarkable advertisement are really doing is giving proof of their psychological perspicacity. They need to overcome the indifference and profound apathy people have in this country when faced with a choice between two entertainments, two jobs, and often, even between two women. One decides only when compelled to do so. And the advertisers are perfectly aware of this. They will go to American extremes, since the same exasperating conditions exist in both places.

Finally, the streets of Oran reveal the two main pleasures of the local young people: having their shoes shined, and promenading in these same shoes along the boulevard. To understand fully the first of these two sensual delights, you must entrust your shoes at ten o'clock on a Sunday morning to the shoe shiners on the boulevard Gallieni. There, perched on a high armchair, one can enjoy the peculiar satisfaction that even the layman derives from the spectacle of men as deeply and visibly in love with their work as are the shoe cleaners of Oran. Everything is worked out to the last detail. Several brushes, three kinds of polishing rags, shoe polish mixed with gasoline: one would think the operation concluded as a perfect shine rises beneath the application of the soft brush. But the same eager hand puts a second coat of polish on the gleaming surface, rubs it, dulls it, drives the cream into the very heart of the leather and then creates, with the same brush, a double and truly definitive shine that flashes forth from the depths.

The marvels thus obtained are then exhibited to the connoisseurs. To really appreciate the pleasures offered by the boulevard, you must attend the costume balls organized by the young people of Oran every evening in the town's main thoroughfares. 'Fashionable' Oranians between the ages of sixteen and twenty model their elegance on American movie stars, disguising themselves every night before dinner. With curly, brilliantined hair flowing from under a felt hat pulled down over the left ear while its brim obliterates the right eye, the neck encircled in a collar generous enough to receive the continuation of the hair, the microscopic knot of the tie held in place by the strictest of pins, a jacket hanging halfway down the thighs and nipped in at the hips, light-colored trousers hanging short, and shoes gleaming above triple soles, these youths click along the sidewalks, sounding their unshakable self-confidence with their steel-tipped shoes. In every detail they attempt to imitate the style, the brashness, the superiority of Mr Clark Gable. This is why, thanks to their rather careless pronunciation, the town's more critical citizens have nicknamed these young men 'The Clarques'.

In any case, the main boulevards of Oran are invaded late every afternoon by an army of amiable adolescents who take the greatest pains to look like gangsters. Since the young girls know they have been destined since birth to marry these tender-hearted ruffians, they too flaunt the make-up and elegance of the great American actresses. The same cynics consequently christen them 'Marlenes'. Thus, when on the evening boulevards the chirping of birds rises from the palm trees to the sky, scores of Clarques and Marlenes meet, and size each other up appreciatively, happy to be alive and to make-believe, indulging for an hour in the bliss of perfect existences. What we are witnessing here, to quote the envious, are meetings of the American delegation. The words reveal the bitterness of those over thirty who have no part in such games. They fail to see these daily congresses of youth and romantic love for what they are – the parliaments of birds one finds in Hindu literature. But no one, on the boulevards of Oran, discusses the problem of Being, or worries about the way to perfection. There is only the fluttering of wings, the flaunting of outspread tails, flirtations between victorious graces, all the rapture of a careless song that fades with the coming of night.

Already I hear Klestakoff: 'We must concern ourselves with higher things.' Alas, he is quite capable of doing so. A little encouragement, and in a few years time he will populate this desert. But, for the time being, a slightly secretive soul can find deliverance in this facile town, with its parade of made-up maidens so incapable of ready-made emotion that the ruse of their borrowed coquetry is immediately uncovered. Concern ourselves with higher things! We would do better to use our eyes: Santa Cruz carved out of the rock, the mountains, the flat sea, the violent wind and the sun, the tall cranes in the docks, the sheds, the quays, and the gigantic flights of stairs that scale the rock on which the town is set, and in the town itself the games and the boredom, the tumult and the solitude. Perhaps none of this is elevated enough. But the great value of such overpopulated islands is that in them the heart can strip itself bare. Silence is possible now only in noisy towns. From Amsterdam, Descartes writes the aging Guez de Balzac, 'I go walking every day in the confusion of a great people, with as much freedom and quiet as you must find in your country lanes.'

*The Minotaur, or Stopping in Oran*

## THE DESERT IN ORAN

Compelled to live facing a glorious landscape, the people of Oran have overcome this formidable handicap by surrounding themselves with extremely ugly buildings. You expect a town opening on the sea, washed and refreshed by the evening breezes. But except for the Spanish district,* you find a city with its back to the sea, built turning in upon itself, like a snail. Oran is a long circular yellow wall, topped by a hard sky. At first, one wanders around the labyrinth, looking for the sea as for Ariadne's sign. But one turns around and around in the stifling yellow streets. In the end, the Oranians are devoured by the Minotaur of boredom. The Oranians have long since stopped wandering. They have let the monster eat them.

No one can know what stone is all about until he has been to Oran. In this dustiest of cities, the pebble is king. It is so much revered that merchants display it in their windows, either as a paperweight or simply for its appearance. People pile them up along the streets, doubtless for pure visual pleasure, since a year later the pile is still there. Things which

---

* And the new boulevard Front-de-Mer.

elsewhere derive their poetry from being green here take on a face of stone. The hundred or so trees that can be found in the business section of the town have been carefully covered with dust. They are a petrified forest, their branches exuding an acrid, dusty smell. In Algiers, the Arab cemeteries have the gentleness they are known for. In Oran, above the Ras-el-Aïn ravine, facing the sea for once, laid out against the blue sky are fields of chalky, crumbly pebbles set blindingly on fire by the sun. In the midst of these dead bones of the earth, here and there a crimson geranium lends its life and fresh blood to the landscape. The whole town is held fast in a stone vice. Seen from the Planters, the cliffs that hold it in their grip are so thick that the landscape loses its reality in so much mineral. Man is an outlaw. So much heavy beauty seems to come from another world.

If one can define the desert as a place with no soul where the sky alone is king, then Oran awaits its prophets. All around and above the town Africa's brutal nature is resplendent in its burning glory. It shatters the ill-chosen décor men have laid upon it, thrusting its violent cries between each house and down on all the rooftops. As one climbs one of the roads along the side of Santa Cruz mountain, what appears at first are the scattered, brightly colored cubes of Oran. A bit higher, and already the jagged

## The Minotaur, or Stopping in Oran

cliffs surrounding the plateau crouch into the sea like red beasts. A little higher still and great whirlpools of sun and wind blanket the untidy town, blowing and battering through its scattered confusion in all four corners of the rocky landscape. Confronted here are man's magnificent anarchy and the permanence of an unchanging sea. Enough to raise along the mountain road a mounting, overwhelming scent of life.

There is something implacable about deserts. The mineral sky of Oran, its trees and streets coated with dust unite to create this thick, impassive world in which the mind and heart are never diverted from themselves or their single subject, which is man. I am speaking here of difficult retreats. People write books about Florence and Athens. These towns have formed so many European minds that they must have a meaning. They maintain the power to sadden or excite. They calm a certain hunger of the soul whose proper food is memory. But how can one feel tender in a town where nothing appeals to the mind, where even ugliness is anonymous, where the past is reduced to nothing? Emptiness, boredom, an indifferent sky: what enticements do these places offer? Solitude, doubt, and perhaps human beings. For a certain race of men, human beings, wherever they are beautiful, are a bitter homeland. Oran is one of the thousand capitals such men possess.

## Sports

The Central Sporting Club, in the rue du Fondouk, in Oran, is presenting an evening of boxing, which it claims will be appreciated by those who really love the sport. What this actually means is that the boxers whose names are on the posters are far from being champions, that some of them will be stepping into the ring for the first time, and that you can therefore count on the courage, if not the skill, of the contestants. Electrified by an Oranian's promise that 'blood will flow', I find myself this evening among the real lovers of the sport.

It would appear that the fans never demand comfort. A ring has been erected at the far end of a kind of whitewashed, garishly lit garage, with a corrugated iron roof. Folding chairs have been set up on all four sides of the ropes. These are the 'ringside seats'. Other seats have been set up the length of the hall, and at the far end there is a wide open space known as the 'promenade', so named because not one of the five hundred people standing there can take out his pocket handkerchief without causing a serious accident. A thousand men and two or three women – of the type who, according to my neighbor, 'always want to show off' – are breathing in this rectangular box. Everyone is sweating ferociously. While we wait for the young hopefuls to step into the ring, an immense loudspeaker grinds out Tino Rossi. Ballads before butchery.

The true fan has limitless patience. The match scheduled for nine o'clock has not yet started at half past, and yet no one complains. It is a warm spring evening, and the smell of men in shirtsleeves is intoxicating. Vigorous discussions are punctuated with the periodic popping of lemonade corks and the tireless lamentations of the Corsican singer. A few late arrivals squeeze into the audience as a spotlight rains blinding light on the ring. The amateur fights begin.

These 'white hopes', or beginners, who fight for pleasure, are always anxious to prove it by massacring each other at the first opportunity, with a fine disregard for technique. None of them has ever lasted more than three rounds. Tonight's hero is a certain 'Kid Avion', who ordinarily sells lottery tickets on café terraces. At the beginning of the second round, his opponent took an unfortunate dive out of the ring under the impact of a propeller-like fist.

## Sports

The crowd has grown a little more excited, though still polite. Gravely, it inhales the sacred scent of liniment. It contemplates this series of slow rites and confused sacrifices, rendered even more authentic by the expiatory patterns thrown against the whiteness of the wall by the struggling shadows. These are the formal prologue of a savage and calculated religion. Only later comes the trance.

And, at this very moment, the loudspeaker introduces Amar, 'the hometown tough who has never surrendered', against Pérez, 'the Algerian puncher'. An outsider might well misinterpret the howls that greet the presentation of the boxers in the ring. He would imagine this was some sensational fight in which the two rivals were going to settle a personal quarrel well known to the public. It is, indeed, a quarrel that they are going to settle, but one that, for the last hundred years, has mortally divided Algiers and Oran. A few hundred years ago, these two North African towns would already have bled each other white, as Florence and Pisa did in happier times. Their rivalry is all the stronger for being based on absolutely nothing. Having every reason to love each other, they hate all the more intensely. The Oranians accuse the Algerians of being 'stuck-up'. The Algerians insinuate that Oranians have no manners. Such insults are more scathing than one might think, since they are metaphysical. And, because they cannot besiege each other, Oran and Algiers meet, struggle, and exchange insults in the field of sport and in competition over statistics and public works.

A page of history is therefore unfolding in the ring. And the hometown tough guy, supported by a thousand howling voices, is defending a way of life and the pride of a province against Pérez. Truth compels me to say that Amar is making his points badly. His arguments are out of order: he lacks reach. The Algerian puncher, on the other hand, is long enough in the arm and makes his points persuasively against his opponent's eyebrow. The Oranian flaunts his colors triumphantly, amid the howls of the frenzied spectators. In spite of repeated encouragement from the gallery and from my neighbor, in spite of the fearless 'Slug him', 'Give him hell', the insidious cries of 'foul', 'Oh, the referee didn't see it', the optimistic 'He's pooped', 'He's had it', the Algerian is declared winner on points to the accompaniment of interminable booing. My neighbor, who likes to talk about the sporting spirit, applauds ostentatiously, whispering to me in a voice hoarse from shouting: 'They won't be able to say *there* that Oranians are rude.'

But in the hall itself a number of unscheduled fights have already broken out. Chairs are brandished in the air, the police force their way through, the excitement is at its height. To calm these good people and contribute to the restoration of silence, the 'management' instantly entrusts the loudspeaker with the thunderous march *Sambre-et-Meuse*. For a few moments the hall takes on a wondrous aspect. Confused bunches of fighters and benevolent referees wave to and fro beneath the policemen's grasp, the gallery is delighted and urges them to further efforts with wild cries, cock-a-doodle-doos, or ironic catcalls soon drowned in the irresistible flood of military music.

But the announcement that the main fight is about to start is enough to restore calm. This happens quickly, with no flourishes, the way actors leave the stage as soon as the play is over. In the most natural way in the world, hats are dusted, chairs put back in their place, and every face immediately assumes the benign expression of the respectable spectator who has paid for his seat at a family concert.

In the last fight of the evening a French naval champion confronts an Oranian boxer. This time it is the latter who has the advantage of reach. But in the first few rounds his superiority does not appeal much to the crowd, which is sleeping off its excitement, convalescing. Everyone is still out of breath. The applause seems unfelt; the whistling half-hearted.

The spectators split into two camps, as they must do if order is to prevail. But each man's choice yields to the indifference of great weariness. If the Frenchman holds in the clinches, if the Oranian forgets that one does not punch with the head, the boxer is bowled over, by a broadside of hisses but immediately put back on his feet with a salvo of applause. It is not until the seventh round that Sport reappears as the fans begin to rouse from their fatigue. The Frenchman has actually hit the canvas and anxious to regain points has charged at his opponent. 'Here we go,' says my neighbor. 'Now comes the bull-fight.' And that is just what it is. Bathed in sweat under the implacable lights, the two boxers open their guard, close their eyes, and swing. They push with their knees and shoulders, exchange blood, and snort with fury. At the same moment, the spectators rise and punctuate each hero's effort. They take the blows, return them, echoing them in a thousand harsh and panting voices. Those who arbitrarily picked their favorite stick stubbornly to their choices, and get passionate about it. Every ten seconds my right ear is pierced by my neighbor's shouting: 'Come on, blue-jacket! Get him, sailor,' while a spectator in front of us shouts '*Anda, hombre!*' to the Oranian. The hombre and the blue-jacket go to it, egged on in this whitewashed temple of cement and corrugated tin

*Sports*

by a crowd completely given over to these low-brow gods. Every dull thud on the gleaming chests echoes in enormous vibrations through the very body of the crowd, who, along with the boxers themselves, give the fight their all.

In this atmosphere, the announcement of a draw is badly received. It runs contrary to what, in the crowd, is an utterly Manichaean vision: there is good and evil, the winner and the loser. One must be right if one isn't wrong. The result of this impeccable logic is immediately expressed by two thousand energetic lungs accusing the judges of being either bought or sold. But the blue-jacket has embraced his opponent in the ring and drinks in his fraternal sweat. This is enough to make the crowd effect an immediate about-face and burst into applause. My neighbor is right: they are not uncivilized.

The crowd spilling out now into a night filled with silence and stars has just fought the most exhausting land of battle. The people say nothing, they slip furtively away, too exhausted for post-mortems. There is good and evil; this religion is merciless. The cohort of the faithful is now nothing more than a bunch of black and white shadows disappearing into the night. Strength and violence are lonely gods; they do not serve memory. They simply scatter their miraculous fistfuls in the present. They correspond to these people without a past who celebrate their communions around the boxing ring. Their rites are a bit trying, but they simplify everything. Good and evil, the winner and the loser: At Corinth, two temples stood side by side – the Temple of Violence, the Temple of Necessity.

MONUMENTS

For many reasons that have as much to do with economy as with metaphysics, one can say that Oranian style, if such a thing exists, finds clear and forceful expression in that singular edifice known as the *Maison du Colon*. Oran is scarcely lacking in monuments. The city has its quota of Imperial Marshals, ministers, and local benefactors. You come across them in little, dusty squares, as resigned to rain as to sun, converted like everything else to stone and boredom. Yet they represent something imported. In this happy barbarity they are unfortunate traces of civilization.

On the other hand, Oran has raised altars and rostrums in its own honor. Needing a building to house the innumerable agricultural organizations that provide the country a livelihood, they decided to erect it in the most solid materials, placing it at the center of the business district, a convincing representation of their virtues: *La Maison du Colon*. Judging from this building, these virtues are three in number: boldness of taste, love of violence, and a sense of historical synthesis. Egypt, Babylon, and Munich have collaborated in this delicate construction – a large cake resembling an immense inverted cup. Multicolored stones are set along each side of the roof, to the most startling effect. The brightness of the mosaic is so persuasive that all one can discern at first is a shapeless dazzle. But closer inspection reveals a meaning to the fully alerted attention: a gracious settler, in bow tie and sun helmet, is receiving the homage of a procession of slaves clad as nature intended.* Finally, the edifice with all these illuminations has been erected at the center of an intersection, amid the bustle of the tiny gondola-shaped tramways whose squalor is one of the town's charms.

Oran is, moreover, very attached to the two lions that stand in its main square. Since 1888 they have sat majestically on either side of the staircase leading up to the town hall. Their creator was named Caïn. They look imperious and are short in the body. It's said that at night they descend one after the other

---

* As one can see, another quality of the Algerian race is candor.

from their pedestals and pad silently around the darkened square, occasionally stopping to urinate thoughtfully beneath the tall, dusty fig trees. These are rumors, of course, to which Oranians lend an indulgent ear. But the whole thing's unlikely.

Despite some research, I have not been able to develop any great enthusiasm for Caïn. All I have discovered is that he enjoyed a reputation as a skillful depicter of animals. Nonetheless, I often think of him – a tendency the mind acquires in Oran. An artist whose name has a certain echo, who gave this town a work of no importance. Several hundred thousand men have grown familiar with the jovial beasts he placed in front of a pretentious town hall. This is one kind of artistic success. These two lions doubtless bear witness, like thousands of works on the same order, to something quite different from talent. Other men were able to create 'The Night Watch', 'Saint Francis Receiving the Stigmata', 'David', or 'The Exaltation of the Flower'. Caïn stuck two grinning cats in the town square of a trading province overseas. But David one day will crumble along with Florence, while these lions perhaps will be saved from disaster. Once again, they hint at something further.

Can I clarify this idea? These statues are both insignificant and solid. The mind has made no contribution

## Sports

to them, matter a very large one. Mediocrity seeks to endure by any means, including bronze. We refuse its claims to eternity, but it makes them every day. Isn't mediocrity itself eternity? In any case, there is something touching about this perseverance; it has its lesson, the lesson offered by all Oran's monuments and by the city itself. For an hour a day, once in a while, you are compelled to take an interest in something that is not important. The mind can profit from such moments of calm. This is how it takes the cure, and because these moments of humility are absolutely necessary to the mind, it seems to me this opportunity for mental relaxation is better than many others. Everything perishable seeks to endure. Let's admit that everything wishes to endure. Man's works have no other meaning, and in this respect Caïn's lions have the same chance of success as the ruins at Angkor. This inclines us to be modest.

There are other monuments in Oran, or, at least, that is what we must call them since they too are representative of their town, in perhaps a more significant way. They are the excavations now being made along the coastline for a distance of ten kilometers. The ostensible reason is to transform the brightest of bays into an enormous port. Actually, it is still another opportunity for man to pit himself against stone.

*Albert Camus*

In the canvases of certain Flemish masters, you see the insistent recurrence of an admirably spacious theme: building the Tower of Babel. There are immense landscapes, rocks reaching up into the sky, escarpments teeming with workmen, animals, ladders, strange machines, ropes, and beams. Man is in the picture only to bring out the inhuman vastness of the construction. This is what comes to mind along the coast west of Oran.

Clinging to immense slopes are rails, pick-up trucks, cranes, and miniature railways . . . Through whistles, dust, and smoke, toylike locomotives twist around vast blocks of stone under a devouring sun. Night and day a nation of ants swarms over the smoking carcass of the mountain. Scores of men, hanging from the same rope against the cliff face, their bellies pressed to the handles of pneumatic drills, quiver day after day in mid-air, unloosing whole patches of stone that crash down in a roar of dust. Further along, trucks dump their loads from the top of the slopes, and the rocks, suddenly launched toward the sea, roll and dive into the water, each heavy block followed by a shower of lighter stones. At regular intervals, in the dead of night or in the middle of the day, explosions shake the whole mountain and raise the very sea itself.

What man is doing with these excavations is launching a head-on attack against stone. And if we

*Sports*

could for a moment forget the harsh slavery that makes this work possible, we would be filled with admiration. These stones, wrenched from the mountain, help man in his designs. They pile up beneath the first waves, gradually emerge, and finally take shape as a jetty that will soon be covered with men and machines daily moving further out to sea. Vast steel jaws gnaw unceasingly at the cliff's belly, swivel round, and disgorge their excess rubble into the sea. As the face of the cliff sinks lower, the whole coast pushes the sea relentlessly backward.

Stone, of course, cannot be destroyed. All one can do is move it around. In any case, it will always outlast the men who use it. For the moment, it supports their determination to act. Even that determination is doubtless quite gratuitous. But to move things around is man's work: he must choose between doing that or doing nothing at all.* Clearly, the Oranians have chosen. For years to come they will keep piling rocks along the coast and into its indifferent bay. In a hundred years, that is to say, tomorrow, they will have to start again. But today these heaps of rock express the men who move in and out among

---

\* This essay deals with one particular temptation. One must have known it. Then one can act or not act, but knowing what the terms are.

them, their faces masked in dust and sweat. The true monuments of Oran are still its stones.

## ARIADNE'S STONE

The people of Oran, it would seem, are like that friend of Flaubert's who, from his deathbed, cast a last look on this irreplaceable earth and cried out: 'Close the window, it's too beautiful.' They have closed the window, they have walled themselves in, they have exorcized the landscape. But Le Poittevin died, and the days continued to follow one another just the same. Just as the sea and land beyond the yellow walls of Oran continue their indifferent dialogue. This permanence in the world has always had a charm for man. It excites him and drives him to despair. The world never has more than one thing to say; it is interesting, then boring. But, in the long run, it triumphs through obstinacy. It is always right.

At the very gates of Oran, nature speaks more insistently. Immense stretches of wasteland, covered with fragrant brush, lie in the direction of Canastel. There, the wind and sun speak only of solitude. Rising over Oran is Santa Cruz Mountain, with its plateau and the thousand ravines leading to it. Roads once traveled by coaches cling against the hillsides overlooking the sea. In January, some are covered with flowers. Buttercups and daisies transform them into sumptuous paths, embroidered in white and yellow. Enough has been said about Santa Cruz. But if I had to describe it, I would forget the sacred processions climbing its harsh slopes on great feast days to evoke other pilgrims who find their way in solitude through the red stones, mounting above the motionless bay, to consecrate one perfect, luminous hour to its bareness.

Oran also has deserts of sand: its beaches. The ones near the city gates are empty only in winter and in spring. They are plateaus then, covered with asphodels, and dotted with small, bare villas among the flowers. Below them growls the sea. Yet the sun, the slight wind, the whiteness of the asphodels, the harsh blue of the sky already foreshadow the summer and the golden youth swarming over the beach, long hours on the sand, and the sudden gentleness of evening. Each year there is a new harvest of flower maidens on these shores. Apparently, they only last the season. The next year other warm blossoms, still little girls with bodies hard as buds the summer before, take their place. Descending from the plateau at eleven in the morning, all this young flesh, scarcely covered by its motley garments, flows across the sand like a multicolored wave.

One must go farther (yet strangely near the place

where two hundred thousand men turn in circles) to find a landscape still virgin: long, empty dunes on which the passage of men has left no other trace than a worm-eaten hut. From time to time, an Arab shepherd leads the black and beige spots of his herd of goats across the top of the dunes. On these beaches in the province of Oran each summer morning feels like the world's first. Each dusk feels like the last, a solemn death proclaimed at sunset by a final light that darkens every shade. The sea is aquamarine, the road the color of dried blood, the beach yellow. Everything vanishes with the green sun; an hour later, the dunes are streaming with moonlight. These are boundless nights beneath a shower of stars. Storms occasionally drift across them, and flashes of lightning shoot along the dunes, turn the sky pale, casting an orange glow upon the sand or in our eyes.

But this cannot be shared in words. It must be lived. So much solitude and grandeur make these places unforgettable. In the mild early dawn, beyond the small, still black and bitter waves, a new being cleaves the scarcely endurable waters of the night. The memory of these joys holds no regret, and that is how I know that they were good. After so many years, they are still there, somewhere in this heart that finds fidelity so difficult. And I know that today, if I want to go back, the same sky will still pour its cargo of stars and breezes upon the deserted dunes. These are the lands of innocence.

But innocence needs sand and stone. And man has forgotten how to live with them. At least, this appears to be the case, since he has enclosed himself in this strange town where boredom slumbers. Yet it is this confrontation which gives Oran its value. The capital of boredom, besieged by innocence and beauty, is hemmed in by an army of as many soldiers as stones. At certain times, though, how tempted one feels in this town to defect to the enemy! How tempting to merge oneself with these stones, to mingle with this burning, impassive universe that challenges history and its agitations! A vain temptation, no doubt. But every man has a deep instinct that is neither for destruction nor creation. Simply the longing to resemble nothing. In the shade of the warm buildings of Oran, on its dusty asphalt, one sometimes hears this invitation. For a while, it seems, minds which yield to it are never disappointed. They have the shades of Eurydice and the sleep of Isis. These are the deserts where thought recovers its strength, the cool hand of evening on a troubled heart. No vigil can be kept upon this Mount of Olives; the mind joins and sanctions the sleeping Apostles. Were they really wrong? They did have their revelation after all.

Think of Sakiamouni in the desert. He spent long years there, crouching motionless and looking up to heaven. The gods themselves envied his wisdom and his fate of stone. Swallows had nested in his stiff and outstretched hands. But, one day, off they flew, following the call of distant lands. And the man who had killed in himself desire and will, glory and sadness, began to weep. And so it is that flowers spring from rock. Yes, let us consent to stone when we must. It too can give us the secret and the rapture that we seek in faces. Of course, it cannot last. But what is there that can? Faces lose their secrets and there we are, reduced once more to the bondage of desire. And if stone can do no more for us than can the human heart, it can at least do just as much.

'To be nothing!' For thousands of years this cry has inspired millions of men to revolt against desire and suffering. Its echoes have traveled over centuries and oceans, coming to rest on the oldest sea in the world. They still reverberate softly against the solid cliffs of Oran. Without knowing it, everyone in this country follows this precept. Of course, it's almost in vain. Nothingness lies within our grasp no more than does the absolute. But since we welcome as evidence of grace the eternal signs revealed in roses or in the suffering of men, let us not reject the rare invitations to sleep the earth offers. These have as much truth as the others.

Here, perhaps, is the Ariadne's thread of this frenzied and somnambulistic city. We acquire the virtues, the wholly provisional virtues, of a certain boredom. To be spared, we must say 'yes' to the Minotaur. It is an ancient, fertile wisdom. Above the sea, lying silent at the foot of the red cliffs, we need only to balance ourselves precisely between the two massive headlands, to the right and to the left, that are washed in the clear water. In the chugging of a coastguard vessel crawling out to sea bathed in radiant light, you can distinctly hear the muffled call of glittering, inhuman forces: the Minotaur's farewell.

It is noon, the day itself stands at a point of balance. His rite accomplished, the traveler receives the price of his deliverance: the little stone, dry and soft as an asphodel, that he picks up on the cliff. For the initiate, the world is no heavier to carry than that stone. The burden of Atlas is easy; all one need do is choose his moment. One realizes then that for an hour, a month, a year, these shores can lend themselves to freedom. They offer the same uncritical welcome to the monk, the civil servant, or the conqueror. There were days when I expected to run into Descartes or Cesare Borgia in the streets of Oran. It didn't happen. But perhaps someone else will be more fortunate than I. A great action, a great undertaking, virile meditation used to call for the solitude of a desert or a convent. It was there that men kept vigil over the weapons of their minds. What better place to keep these vigils now than in the emptiness of a large town built to last a long time in the midst of mindless beauty?

Here is the small stone, soft as an asphodel. It lies at the beginning of everything. Flowers, tears (if you insist), departures and struggles are for tomorrow. In the middle of the journey, when the heavens open their fountains of light into vast, resounding space, the headlands all along the coast look like a fleet of ships impatient to weigh anchor. These heavy galleons of rock and light tremble on their keels as if in preparation for a voyage to the island of the sun. Oh, the mornings in Oran! From high on the plateaus, the swallows swoop down into the immense cauldrons of simmering air. The whole coast is ready for departure, a thrill of adventure runs along it. Tomorrow, perhaps, we shall set sail together.

1939

## *A Short Guide to Towns Without a Past*

The softness of Algiers is rather Italian. The cruel glare of Oran has something Spanish about it. Constantine, perched high on a rock above the Rummel Gorges, is reminiscent of Toledo. But Spain and Italy overflow with memories, with works of art and exemplary ruins. Toledo has had its El Greco and its Barrès. The cities I speak of, on the other hand, are towns without a past. Thus they are without tenderness or abandon. During the boredom of the siesta hours, their sadness is implacable and has no melancholy. In the morning light, or in the natural luxury of the evenings, their delights are equally ungentle. These towns give nothing to the mind and everything to the passions. They are suited neither to wisdom nor to the delicacies of taste. A Barrès or anyone like him would be completely pulverized.

Travelers with a passion for other people's passions, oversensitive souls, aesthetes, and newlyweds have nothing to gain from going to Algiers. And, unless he had a divine call, a man would be ill-advised to retire and live there forever. Sometimes, in Paris, when people I respect ask me about Algeria, I feel like crying out: 'Don't go there.' Such joking has some truth in it. For I can see what they are expecting and know they will not find it. And, at the same time, I know the attractions and the subtle power of this country, its insinuating hold on those who linger, how it immobilizes them first by ridding them of questions and finally by lulling them to sleep with its everyday life. At first the revelation of the light, so glaring that everything turns black and white, is almost suffocating. One gives way to it, settles down in it, and then realizes that this protracted splendor gives nothing to the soul and is merely an excessive delight. Then one would like to return to the mind. But the men of this country – and this is their strength – seem to have more heart than mind. They can be your friends (and what friends!), but you can never tell them your secrets. This might be considered dangerous here in Paris, where souls are poured out so extravagantly and where the water of secrets flows softly and endlessly along among the fountains, the statues, and the gardens.

This land most resembles Spain. With no traditions Spain would be merely a beautiful desert. And unless one happens to have been born there, there is

## A Short Guide to Towns Without a Past

only one race of men who can dream of withdrawing forever to the desert. Having been born in this desert, I can hardly think of describing it as a visitor. Can one catalogue the charms of a woman one loves dearly? No, one loves her all of a piece, if I may use the expression, with one or two precise reasons for tenderness, like a favorite pout or a particular way of shaking the head. Such is my long-standing liaison with Algeria, one that will doubtless never end and that keeps me from being completely lucid. All anyone can do in such a case is to persevere and make a kind of abstract list of what he loves in the thing he loves. This is the kind of academic exercise I can attempt here on the subject of Algeria.

First there is the beauty of the young people. The Arabs, of course, and then the others. The French of Algeria are a bastard race, made up of unexpected mixtures. Spaniards and Alsatians, Italians, Maltese, Jews, and Greeks have met here. As in America, such raw intermingling has had happy results. As you walk through Algiers, look at the wrists of the women and the young men, and then think of the ones you see in the Paris *métro*.

The traveler who is still young will also notice that the women are beautiful. The best place in Algiers to appreciate this is the terrace of the Café des Facultés, in the rue Michelet, on a Sunday morning in

April. Groups of young women in sandals and light, brightly colored dresses walk up and down the street. You can admire them without inhibitions: that is what they come for. The Cintra bar, on the boulevard Galliéni in Oran, is also a good observatory. In Constantine, you can always stroll around the bandstand. But since the sea is several hundred kilometers away, there is something missing in the people you meet there. In general, and because of this geographical location, Constantine offers fewer attractions, although the quality of its ennui is rather more delicate.

If the traveler arrives in summer, the first thing to do, obviously, is to go down to the beaches surrounding the towns. He will see the same young people, more dazzling because less clothed. The sun gives them the somnolent eyes of great beasts. In this respect, the beaches of Oran are the finest, for both nature and women are wilder there.

As for the picturesque, Algiers offers an Arab town, Oran a Negro village and a Spanish district, and Constantine a Jewish quarter. Algiers has a long necklace of boulevards along the sea; you must walk there at night. Oran has few trees, but the most beautiful stone in the world. Constantine has a suspension bridge where the thing to do is have your photograph taken. On very windy days, the

## A Short Guide to Towns Without a Past

bridge sways to and fro above the deep gorges of the Rummel, and you have the feeling of danger.

I recommend that the sensitive traveler, if he goes to Algiers, drink *anisette* under the archways around the harbor, go to La Pêcherie in the morning and eat freshly caught fish grilled on charcoal stoves; listen to Arab music in a little café on the rue de la Lyre whose name I've forgotten; sit on the ground, at six in the evening, at the foot of the statue of the duc d'Orléans, in Government Square (not for the sake of the duke, but because there are people walking by, and it's pleasant there); have lunch at Padovani's, which is a kind of dance hall on stilts along the seashore, where the life is always easy; visit the Arab cemeteries, first to find calm and beauty there, then to appreciate at their true value the ignoble cities where we stack our dead; go and smoke a cigarette in the Casbah on the rue des Bouchers, in the midst of spleens, livers, lungs, and intestines that drip blood on everything (the cigarette is necessary, these medieval practices have a strong smell).

As to the rest, you must be able to speak ill of Algiers when in Oran (insist on the commercial superiority of Oran's harbor), make fun of Oran when in Algiers (don't hesitate to accept the notion that Oranians 'don't know how to live'), and, at every opportunity, humbly acknowledge the surpassing merit of Algiers in comparison to metropolitan France. Once these concessions have been made, you will be able to appreciate the real superiority of the Algerian over the Frenchman – that is to say, his limitless generosity and his natural hospitality.

And now perhaps I can stop being ironic. After all, the best way to speak of what one loves is to speak of it lightly. When Algeria is concerned, I am always afraid to pluck the inner cord it touches in me, whose blind and serious song I know so well. But at least I can say that it is my true country, and that anywhere in the world I recognize its sons and my brothers by the friendly laughter that fills me at the sight of them. Yes, what I love about the cities of Algeria is not separate from their inhabitants. That is why I like it best there in the evening when the shops and offices pour into the still, dim streets a chattering crowd that runs right up to the boulevards facing the sea and starts to grow silent there, as night falls and the lights from the sky, from the lighthouses in the bay, and from the streetlamps merge together little by little into a single flickering glow. A whole people stands meditating on the seashore then, a thousand solitudes springing up from the crowd. Then the vast African nights begin, the royal exile, and the celebration of despair that awaits the solitary traveler.

No, you must certainly not go there if you have

a lukewarm heart or if your soul is weak and weary! But for those who know what it is to be torn between yes and no, between noon and midnight, between revolt and love, and for those who love funeral pyres along the shore, a flame lies waiting in Algeria.

1947

## Return to Tipasa

*You sailed away from your father's dwelling*
*With your heart on fire, Medea! And you passed*
*Between the rocky gates of the seas;*
*And now you sleep on a foreign shore.*

*– Medea*

For five days the rain had been falling unceasingly on Algiers, finally drenching the sea itself. From the heights of an apparently inexhaustible sky, unending sheets of rain, so thick they were viscous, crashed into the gulf. Soft and gray like a great sponge, the sea heaved in the shapeless bay. But the surface of the water seemed almost motionless beneath the steady rain. At long intervals, however, a broad and imperceptible movement raised a murky cloud of steam from the sea and rolled it into the harbor, below a circle of soaking boulevards. The town itself, its white walls running with damp, gave off another cloud of steam that billowed out to meet the first. Whichever way you turned you seemed to be breathing water, you could drink the very air.

Looking at this drowned sea, seeing in December an Algiers that was still for me the city of summers, I walked about and waited. I had fled from the night of Europe, from a winter of faces. But even the town of summers was emptied of its laughter, offering me only hunched and streaming backs. In the evening, in the fiercely lit cafés where I sought refuge, I read my age on faces I recognized without knowing their names. All I knew was that these men had been young when I was, and that now they were young no longer.

I stayed on, though, without any clear idea of what I was waiting for, except, perhaps, the moment when I could go back to Tipasa. It is certainly a great folly, and one that is almost always punished, to go back to the places of one's youth, to want to relive at forty the things one loved or greatly enjoyed at twenty. But I was aware of this folly. I had already been back to Tipasa once, not long after those war years that marked for me the end of my youth. I hoped, I think, to rediscover there a liberty I was unable to forget. Here, more than twenty years ago, I had spent whole mornings wandering among the ruins, breathing the scent of absinthe, warming myself against the stones, discovering the tiny, short-lived roses that survive in springtime. Only at noon, when even the crickets are silenced by the heat, would I flee from the avid blaze of an all-consuming light. Sometimes, at night, I would sleep open-eyed beneath a sky flowing with stars. I was alive at those moments. Fifteen years later, I found my ruins again. A few steps from the first waves, I followed the streets of the forgotten city across the fields covered with bitter trees; and, on the hills overlooking the bay, could still caress their pillars, which were the color of bread. But now the ruins were surrounded by barbed wire, and could be reached only through official entrances. It was also forbidden, for reasons sanctioned, it would seem, by morality, to walk there after dark; by day, one would meet an official guard. That morning, doubtless by chance, it was raining across the whole sweep of the ruins.

Bewildered, walking through the lonely, rain-soaked countryside, I tried at least to recover the strength that has so far never failed me, that helps me to accept what is, once I have realized I cannot change it. I could not, of course, travel backward through time and restore to this world the face I had loved, which had disappeared in a single day a long time before. On the second of September, 1939, I did not go to Greece, as I had planned. Instead, the war enveloped us, then Greece itself.

This distance, these years separating the warm ruins from the barbed wire, were also within me, as I stood that day staring at tombs filled with black water or beneath the dripping tamarisk trees. Raised above all in the spectacle of a beauty that was my only wealth, I had begun in plenty. The barbed wire came later – I mean tyrannies, war, policings, the time of revolt. We had had to come to terms with night: the beauty of daytime was only a memory. And in this muddy Tipasa, even the memory was growing dim. No room now for beauty, fullness, or youth! In the light cast by the flames, the world had suddenly shown its wrinkles and its afflictions, old and new. It had suddenly grown old, and we had too. I knew the ardor I had come in search of could only be roused in someone not expecting it. There is no love without a little innocence. Where was innocence? Empires were crumbling, men and nations were tearing at one another's throats; our mouths were dirtied. Innocent at first without knowing it, now we were unintentionally guilty: the more we knew, the greater the mystery. This is why we busied ourselves, oh mockery, with morality. Frail in spirit, I dreamed of virtue! In the days of innocence, I did not know morality existed. Now I knew it did, and could not live up to it. On the promontory I had loved in former days, between the drenched pillars

## Return to Tipasa

of the ruined temple, I seemed to be walking behind someone whose footsteps I could still hear on the tombstones and mosaics, but whom I would never catch up with again. I went back to Paris, and stayed for some years before returning home again.

During all these years, however, I had a vague feeling of missing something. Once you have had the chance to love intensely, your life is spent in search of the same light and the same ardor. To give up beauty and the sensual happiness that comes with it and devote one's self exclusively to unhappiness requires a nobility I lack. But, after all, nothing is true that compels us to make it exclusive. Isolated beauty ends in grimaces, solitary justice in oppression. Anyone who seeks to serve the one to the exclusion of the other serves no one, not even himself, and in the end is doubly the servant of injustice. A day comes when, because we have been inflexible, nothing amazes us any more, everything is known, and our life is spent in starting again. It is a time of exile, dry lives, dead souls. To come back to life, we need grace, a homeland, or to forget ourselves. On certain mornings, as we turn a corner, an exquisite dew falls on our heart and then vanishes. But the freshness lingers, and this, always, is what the heart needs. I had to come back once again.

And, in Algiers a second time, still walking under

the same downpour that I felt had not stopped since what I thought was my final departure, in the midst of this immense melancholy smelling of rain and sea, in spite of the misty sky, the sight of people's backs fleeing beneath the deluge, the cafés whose sulphurous light decomposed everyone's face, I persisted in my hopes. Anyway, didn't I know that rain in Algiers, although it looks as if it would go on forever, nonetheless does stop suddenly, like the rivers in my country that swell to a flood in two hours, devastate acres of land, and dry up again in an instant? One evening, in fact, the rain stopped. I waited still one more night. A liquid morning rose, dazzling, over the pure sea. From the sky, fresh as a rose, washed and rewashed by the waters, reduced by each successive laundering to its most delicate and clearest texture, a quivering light fell, endowing each house, each tree, with a palpable shape and a magic newness. The earth must have risen in just such a light the morning the world was born. Once again I set out for Tipasa.

There is not a single one of these sixty-nine kilometers of highway that is not filled for me with memories and sensations. A violent childhood, adolescent daydreams to the hum of the bus's engines, mornings, the freshness of young girls, beaches, young muscles always tensed, the slight anguish

## Return to Tipasa

that the evening brings to a sixteen-year-old heart, the desire to live, glory, and always the same sky, for months on end, with its inexhaustible strength and light, as companion to the years, a sky insatiable, one by one devouring victims lying crucified upon the beach at the funereal hour of noon. Always the same sea as well, almost impalpable in the morning air, glimpsed again on the horizon as soon as the road, leaving the Sahel and its hills with their bronze-colored vineyards, dipped down toward the coast. But I did not stop to look at it. I wanted to see the Chenoua again – that heavy, solid mountain, carved all in one piece and running along the west side of Tipasa Bay before descending into the sea. You see it from far away, long before you get there, as a light blue haze still mingling with the sea. But gradually it condenses as you come nearer, until it takes on the color of the waters surrounding it, like an immense and motionless wave brutally caught in the very act of breaking over a suddenly calm sea. Nearer still, almost at the gates of Tipasa, you see its frowning mass, brown and green, the old, unshakable, moss-covered god, port and haven for its sons, of whom I am one. I was gazing at it as I finally crossed the barbed wire and stood among the ruins. And, in the glorious December light, as happens only once or twice in lives that may later be described as heaped with every blessing, I found exactly what I had come in search of, something which in spite of time and in spite of the world was offered to me and truly to me alone, in this deserted nature. From the olive-strewn forum, one could see the village down below. Not a sound came from it; wisps of smoke rose in the limpid air. The sea also lay silent, as if breathless beneath the unending shower of cold, glittering light. From the Chenoua, a distant cock crow alone sang the fragile glory of the day. Across the ruins, as far as one could see, there were nothing but pitted stones and absinthe plants, trees and perfect columns in the transparence of the crystal air. It was as if the morning stood still, as if the sun had stopped for an immeasurable moment. In this light and silence, years of night and fury melted slowly away. I listened to an almost forgotten sound within myself, as if my heart had long been stopped and was now gently beginning to beat again. And, now awake, I recognized one by one the imperceptible sounds that made up the silence: the *basso continuo* of the birds, the short, light sighing of the sea at the foot of the rocks, the vibration of the trees, the blind song of the columns, the whispering of the absinthe plants, the furtive lizards. I heard all this, and also felt the waves of happiness rising up within me. I felt that I had at last come back to harbor, for a moment at least, and that from now on this moment would never end. But soon afterward the sun rose visibly a degree higher in the sky. A blackbird chirped its brief prelude and immediately, from all around, bird voices exploded with a strength, a jubilation, a joyful discord, an infinite delight. The day moved on. It was to carry me through till evening.

At noon, on the half-sandy slopes, strewn with heliotropes like a foam that the furious waves of the last few days had left behind in their retreat, I gazed at the sea, gently rising and falling as if exhausted, and quenched two thirsts that cannot be long neglected if all one's being is not to dry up, the thirst to love and the thirst to admire. For there is only misfortune in not being loved; there is misery in not loving. All of us, today, are dying of this misery. This is because blood and hatred lay bare the heart itself; the long demand for justice exhausts even the love that gave it birth. In the clamor we live in, love is impossible and justice not enough. That is why Europe hates the daylight and can do nothing but confront one injustice with another. In order to prevent justice from shriveling up, from becoming nothing but a magnificent orange with a dry, bitter pulp, I discovered one must keep a freshness and a source of joy intact within, loving the daylight that injustice leaves unscathed, and returning to the fray with this light as a trophy. Here, once more, I found an ancient beauty, a young sky, and measured my good fortune as I realized at last that in the worst years of our madness the memory of this sky had never left me. It was this that in the end had saved me from despair. I had always known that the ruins of Tipasa were younger than our drydocks or our debris. In Tipasa, the world is born again each day in a light always new. Oh light! The cry of all the characters in classical tragedy who come face to face with their destinies. I knew now that their final refuge was also ours. In the depths of winter, I finally learned that within me there lay an invincible summer.

Once more I left Tipasa, returning to Europe and its struggles. But the memory of that day sustains me still and helps me meet both joy and sorrow with equanimity. In the difficult times we face, what more can I hope for than the power to exclude nothing and to learn to weave from strands of black and white one rope tautened to the breaking point? In everything I've done or said so far, I seem to recognize these two forces, even when they contradict each other. I have not been able to deny the light into which I was born and yet I have not wished to reject the responsibilities of our time. It would be too easy to set against the gentle name Tipasa other names

*Return to Tipasa*

more sonorous and more cruel: there is, for man today, an inner path that I know well from having traveled both ways upon it, which leads from the summits of the mind to the capitals of crime. And, doubtless, one can always rest, sleep on the hillside or settle into crime. But if we give up a part of what exists, we must ourselves give up being; we must then give up living or loving except by proxy. Thus there is a will to live without refusing anything life offers: the virtue I honor most in this world. From time to time, at least, it's true that I would like to have practised it. Since few times require to the extent ours does that one be as equal to the best as to the worst, to avoid nothing and keep a double memory alive is precisely what I would like to do. Yes, there is beauty and there are the humiliated. Whatever difficulties the enterprise may present, I would like never to be unfaithful either to the one or the other.

But this still sounds like ethics, and we live for something that transcends ethics. If we could name it, what silence would follow! East of Tipasa, the hill of Sainte-Salsa, evening has come to life. It is still light, of course, but an invisible waning of the light announces the sunset. A wind rises, gentle as the night, and suddenly the untroubled sea chooses its way and flows like a great barren river across the horizon. The sky darkens. Then begins the mystery, the gods of night, and what lies beyond pleasure. But how can this be expressed? The little coin I carry back from here has one clear side, the face of a beautiful woman that reminds me of what I've learned in the course of this day, while the other side, which I feel beneath my fingers homeward bound, has been eaten away. What does this lipless mouth express if not what another, mysterious voice within me says, that daily teaches me my ignorance and my happiness:

> The secret I am looking for is buried in a valley of olive trees, beneath the grass and cold violets, around an old house that smells of vines. For more than twenty years I have wandered over this valley, and over others like it, questioning dumb goatherds, knocking at the door of empty ruins. Sometimes, when the first star shines in a still, clear sky, beneath a rain of delicate light, I have thought that I knew. I did know, in fact. Perhaps I still know. But no one is interested in this secret, doubtless I myself do not desire it, and I cannot cut myself off from my own people. I live with my family, who believe they reign over rich and hideous cities, built of stones and mists.

*Return to Tipasa*

Day and night it raises its voice, and everything yields beneath it while it bows down to nothing: it is deaf to all secrets. Its power sustains me and yet bores me, and I come to be weary of its cries. But its unhappiness is my own, we are of the same blood. I too am sick, and am I not a noisy accomplice who has cried out among the stones? Thus I try to forget, I march through our cities of iron and fire, I smile bravely at the night, I welcome the storms, I will be faithful. In fact, I have forgotten: henceforth, I shall be deaf and active. But perhaps one day, when we are ready to die of ignorance and exhaustion, I shall be able to renounce our shrieking tombs, to go and lie down in the valley, under the unchanging light, and learn for one last time what I know.

1953

PENGUIN ARCHIVE

H. G. Wells *The Time Machine*
M. R. James *The Stalls of Barchester Cathedral*
Jane Austen *The History of England by a Partial, Prejudiced and Ignorant Historian*
Edgar Allan Poe *Hop-Frog*
Virginia Woolf *The New Dress*
Antoine de Saint-Exupéry *Night Flight*
Oscar Wilde *A Poet Can Survive Everything But a Misprint*
George Orwell *Can Socialists be Happy?*
Dorothy Parker *Horsie*
D. H. Lawrence *Odour of Chrysanthemums*
Homer *The Wrath of Achilles*
Emily Brontë *No Coward Soul Is Mine*
Romain Gary *Lady L.*
Charles Dickens *The Chimes*
Dante *Hell*
Georges Simenon *Stan the Killer*
F. Scott Fitzgerald *The Rich Boy*
Katherine Mansfield *A Dill Pickle*
Fyodor Dostoyevsky *The Dream of a Ridiculous Man*

Franz Kafka *A Hunger-Artist*
Leo Tolstoy *Family Happiness*
Karen Blixen *The Dreaming Child*
Federico García Lorca *Cicada!*
Vladimir Nabokov *Revenge*
Albert Camus *A Short Guide to Towns Without a Past*
Muriel Spark *The Driver's Seat*
Carson McCullers *Reflections in a Golden Eye*
Wu Cheng'en *Monkey King Makes Havoc in Heaven*
Friedrich Nietzsche *Ecce Homo*
Laurie Lee *A Moment of War*
Roald Dahl *Lamb to the Slaughter*
Frank O'Connor *The Genius*
James Baldwin *The Fire Next Time*
Hermann Hesse *Strange News from Another Planet*
Gertrude Stein *Paris France*
Seneca *Why I am a Stoic*
Snorri Sturluson *The Prose Edda*
Elizabeth Gaskell *Lois the Witch*
Sei Shōnagon *A Lady in Kyoto*
Yasunari Kawabata *Thousand Cranes*
Jack Kerouac *Tristessa*
Arthur Schnitzler *A Confirmed Bachelor*
Chester Himes *All God's Chillun Got Pride*

Bram Stoker *The Burial of the Rats*
Czesław Miłosz *Rescue*
Hans Christian Andersen *The Emperor's New Clothes*
Bohumil Hrabal *Closely Watched Trains*
Italo Calvino *Under the Jaguar Sun*
Stanislaw Lem *The Seventh Voyage*
Shirley Jackson *The Daemon Lover*
Stefan Zweig *Chess*
Kate Chopin *The Story of an Hour*
Allen Ginsberg *Sunflower Sutra*
Rabindranath Tagore *The Broken Nest*
Søren Kierkegaard *The Seducer's Diary*
Mary Shelley *Transformation*
Nikolai Leskov *Night Owls*
Willa Cather *A Lost Lady*
Emilia Pardo Bazán *The Lady Bandit*
W. B. Yeats *Sailing to Byzantium*
Margaret Cavendish *The Blazing World*
Lafcadio Hearn *Some Japanese Ghosts*
Sarah Orne Jewett *The Country of the Pointed Firs*
Vincent van Gogh *For Art and for Life*
Dylan Thomas *Do Not Go Gentle Into That Good Night*
Mikhail Bulgakov *A Dog's Heart*
Saadat Hasan Manto *The Price of Freedom*

Gérard de Nerval *October Nights*
Rumi *Where Everything is Music*
H. P. Lovecraft *The Shadow Out of Time*
Christina Rossetti *To Read and Dream*
Dambudzo Marechera *The House of Hunger*
Andy Warhol *Beauty*
Maurice Leblanc *The Escape of Arsène Lupin*
Eileen Chang *Jasmine Tea*
Irmgard Keun *After Midnight*
Walter Benjamin *Unpacking My Library*
Epictetus *Whatever is Rational is Tolerable*
Ota Pavel *How I Came to Know Fish*
César Aira *An Episode in the Life of a Landscape Painter*
Hafez *I am a Bird from Paradise*
Clarice Lispector *The Burned Sinner and the Harmonious Angels*
Maryse Condé *Tales from the Heart*
Audre Lorde *Coal*
Mary Gaitskill *Secretary*
Tove Ditlevsen *The Umbrella*
June Jordan *Passion*
Antonio Tabucchi *Requiem*
Alexander Lernet-Holenia *Baron Bagge*
Wang Xiaobo *The Maverick Pig*